TELL ME A STORY

Mia Dalia

CONTENTS

For Chelsea,

who always asks me to

Tell Me a Story

I wake up to a night so dark that for a moment it takes my breath away. I don't know what woke me up, maybe nothing did. It's pitch black. The stygian darkness of horror movies and nightmares. It takes me a moment to orient myself, to gather my thoughts, to calm down, and then, of course, I remember I'm okay, I'm safe, I'm where I'm meant to be— the backroom of Mr. B's Story Emporium bookstore.

It's where I sleep every night now, ever since Mr. B had so generously offered it to me. It has no windows, but I told him I didn't need to see the world all the time. I've had enough of the outside world to last a lifetime. It has a lamp, though, a small metal lamp that sits beside my mattress on a side-turned wooden crate that functions as my nightstand. I locate it by touch and turn it on. And just like that, the darkness is dispelled.

I take a calming breath and look around. All is as it should be, as I left it—the crates neatly stacked in the corner containing my clothes, a box fan, my shoes by the door, my jacket hanging off the hook above them, an old rocking chair, a discard from the bookstore I fixed up to rock again, however unevenly and creakily, is sitting still, a worn blanket tossed over it. The night's too hot for a blanket. I even thought of putting a fan on but must have fallen asleep before I did it. My small kitchen setup takes up an entire far wall, a sink, a countertop with a single hot plate burner, shelves above and below, a mini fridge with a microwave atop of it. All you need to eat alone. My makeshift shower is next to it.

The book I was reading before bed is splayed spine up on my makeshift nightstand. Mr. B would not approve. I pick it up, place a bookmark in it and carefully close it. Mr. B says objects ought to be treated with respect, because it demonstrates to us and to the world what sort of people we are. It's about more than just appearances, though, it's about the way you present yourself, to you, and to the world. It's why I make sure I stay clean and wash my clothes regularly. Small things that dropped out of habit while I was on the streets, small things that I've laboriously reinstated into my routine.

If I am to be a bookseller, I must be presentable. It is, after all, a venerable position. A dying art, says Mr. B. Can't make a living out of it. There's a joke in there somewhere, I know it. Mr. B says my sense of humor needs work. He gives me books to read, to test my funny bone, as he puts it. I'm currently making my way through Christopher Moore's back catalog. It's funny, I like it. I recognize funny, I'm just never quite sure how to do it myself.

I check my watch. It's nearly morning. No point in falling asleep—the day's about to begin. I never liked sleeping. Well, maybe when I was young, but as an adult, it always felt like a waste of time. First, I was so busy with life that I didn't want to miss out on even a minute of it, and then, I had nothing but time, but no safe place to lay my head and relax. I've learned to make do with naps, stolen here and there, or sleep in short intervals.

My current setup is positively luxurious by comparison to what I've gotten used to, but old habits die hard, and I'm still nowhere near the conventionally recommended seven to eight hours.

I get up and do my stretches. It's important to stay limber, to stay fit. I do sit-ups and push-ups; I alternate between the two. I shadowbox. I bet it looks silly. I'm glad there's no one to see me do it. I don't think I could ever box with a real person; I just like the motions. Maybe it's all the *Rocky* movies I watched when I was young.

There's no proper bathroom downstairs, only a ramshackle afterthought of a bathroom about the size of the closet it must have been converted from, with a "Staff Only" sign above it. Makes you think that this is a much larger operation, but there's no staff outside of Mr. B and me. The bathroom is where I wash up in the morning, make myself presentable for the day. I shave, put wet fingers through my short hair, wash my face. Use deodorant. I shower every other day; I have a system. A large metal trough found on the street and cleaned up, a hula-hoop attached to the ceiling above it with a shower curtain treaded through, and an adjustable hose that can connect to my kitchen sink. Voila, a shower. You'd be surprised the tricks you'll learn living on the streets with public bathrooms being your only option. Here, I have the luxury of privacy *and* reliable hot water. It's grand.

Back in my room, I dress. My current wardrobe consists almost exclusively of Mr. B's hand-me-downs. Well-made and well-worn button-down shirts, sweaters, and chinos. All a reasonably good fit, though I'm slightly taller and skinnier. My shoes are an old pair of classic Chuck Taylors I found on the street, just sitting outside on someone's stoop, seemingly waiting for me. The things people throw away … It's how I came by my jacket too, but these days it's too mild for a jacket. Unseasonably so. Indian Summer, they call it. I don't know why. No one ever says Indian Winter, no matter how warm a winter day might be.

I'm ready to face the world now. I don't lock my room—there is no lock and nothing to steal. In fact, there isn't even a way to tell my room is there, the way the store's set up. I live behind the genre fiction section. Science fiction, thrillers, and horror. Quite the company.

There's some extra stock kept behind the shelves, and my room is behind that. No one notices it, and there is no need to, since the store has plenty of stock on the shelves.

I like the people who browse genre fiction. They are invariably an interesting bunch. Often along the lines of a garden variety of nerds and geeks, sure, but it beats the pretentious types that haunt the poetry and plays stacks. Besides, they make for a much more interesting conversation than the women's fiction/romance lovers.

I walk the aisles of the store with something approaching pride. None of this is mine, but I'm the designated caretaker here. It is because of me that the floors are swept and washed, the shelves are dust-free, and the windows are clean. It is because of my efforts that the books sit neatly on their shelves, alphabetized and categorized.

Mr. B needs me for all these things. He has limited mobility. Some condition he won't talk about. He jokes—I think—that it's for all his sins. He gets around alright for now with his cane, but some days he requires two of them, and I know his condition is deteriorating, albeit slowly. Eventually, he'll end up in a wheelchair. We'll have to widen the aisles, I suppose.

Here he comes now. I hear the rapping of his cane. They are all rubber-tipped, but still make that distinct noise as if warning of his approach. Mr. B lives upstairs in an apartment, by himself. I don't know if there was ever a Mrs. B. I don't think so. He seems like a solitary type. There'sa self-sufficiency about him that is usually instilled by years of being on your own.

He brings me breakfast every morning. Mr. B himself only ever has coffee; says he's got no appetite in the morning. For me, he brings a cup of black coffee strong enough to raise the dead, a couple of Pop-Tarts, and an apple. Oslo breakfast, he calls it. I had to ask at first and he explained that it was a type of uncooked school meal developed in Norway in the 1920s and rolled out as a free universal provision for Oslo school children in 1932. Went on for a long time apparently with great success. Produced generations of strong tall Norwegians.

I said I didn't know they had Pop-Tarts in Norway back then, and he laughed and told me they used bread and margarine. I'm glad Mr. B has Pop-Tarts, though. It's a delicious way to start the day and get the blood sugar rushing.

Oslo breakfast is just one of the random obscure facts Mr.

B knows. In fact, he knows tons of them. He'd kill on Jeopardy. Or at a pub quiz. But then, he doesn't get out much these days. I love the things he knows, how vast his knowledge is, the breadth of the subjects it spans. The things he remembers. I wish I was more like that, but truth be told I was never that good at school, and odds are all the damage I did to my brain cells in the subsequent years with various substances hasn't helped.

While I have my breakfast, Mr. B turns the sign on the door to "Open" and unlocks. He loves doing that every morning. Then he takes to his throne, as he affectionately calls the comfy and worn upholstered chair behind the register. Every morning we make a bet on how much business we'll do that day. It's perfectly arbitrary most days, especially if weather isn't a factor.

In the time I've been here, I have learned that the book business is completely unpredictable. Sometimes I'm surprised people even buy books still, what with all the ereaders out there and all the other technological distractions. You'd think books would become obsolete, like records. The record shop in the neighborhood went under years ago. And yet every so often someone comes in and swears that paper books are the only way to go and buys some to prove it. Mr. B attributes this to the nostalgia factor. People long for the past. Strange, considering how eagerly they are immersing themselves in the present, but hey, whatever sells books. Whatever keeps the lights on.

To be fair, I don't know if book sales alone are responsible for the Story Emporium staying in business. Mr. B likes to refer to himself as a gentleman bookseller. He makes it sound as if it's more of a hobby than a livelihood and, if my math is something to go by, a hobby is more like it. In my mind, he had the money upon retirement and decided to invest it into the store. I believe he owns the building outright, and it must be a considerable relief not to have to depend on the book sales alone for his living expenses.

How I came to be here is a different story. I saved Mr. B's life. According to him, anyway. It was altogether much more prosaic than that. Much more of a right time, right place situation. I was sleeping in the alley behind the Story Emporium. It was one of the alleys I liked to sleep in. The town was rife with them, but some were safer than others. Mr. B was taking out the trash late at night when he slipped and fell. This was in the early days of his condition acting up, the days when he still, for reasons of pride or otherwise, tried doing most things without a cane. So, he slipped and hit his head and, we were told later, that if I hadn't been there to help him, to grab his cell phone and call 911, to stay with him, to put my old blanket on him to make sure he was warm, that he probably wouldn't have made it.

When Mr. B came back home, at last, with nothing but a scar and some shaken confidence to show for his fall, he found me and took me in. The best thing that's happened to me in a very, very long time.

There were rules, of course, there were rules. Mr. B is all about rules and regulations. And so, I got clean and sober and managed to stay that way. The drink was the hardest thing to give up, but I was motivated by the promise of a new start and long-forgotten creature comforts and managed.

Now here we are, years later. Funny how the time goes by when you're not thinking about it.

"What say you, youngblood?" Mr. B always calls me funny names. Says my name doesn't fit me. He's probably right. I haven't looked like a Jared since high school. Jared seems like someone taller and happier, someone with more confidence and more muscles.

"Slow morning, followed by a lunch rush and a middling evening, with daily totals approaching but not exceeding 200s."

"Ouch."

"Your turn."

"Well, cynics be damned, an evening rush, total 347."

"347?"

"Why not?" He smiles.

Mr. B has a smile so tight it's a blink-and-you-miss-it sort of thing. Not a jolly old man by any means, he is lean and squinty-eyed and, despite his advanced years, really strong-looking. Not especially tall or imposing, but with a powerful presence. Not a man you'd mess with even now, and I'm sure back in the day he must have been a formidable force. Unlike so many old men I see in the store, Mr. B still has all his hair, it's not grey, it's perfectly white and always neatly brushed back. He has a white beard and mustache to match, the combination of which is heavy enough to almost completely obscure the entire bottom half of his face. He wears glasses with thick black frames and favors a combination of light blue or white button-downs with chinos and comfy grey cardigans. All told, Mr. B looks like a retired college professor, but maybe someone who's also been in the army, smart and not to be messed with.

He can be charming. Women of all ages tend to leave with more books than they planned on buying. He's knowledgeable and funny and makes them laugh. I wish I had that sort of charm. It's such an elusive quality.

Mr. B says to concentrate on the things I can improve and work on those, hence I read and exercise and mind my manners. Manners are important, according to Mr. B they can open every door. Politeness is a sort of key to the world. People can be disarmed by it, taken in. Being polite is the easiest dangerous thing one can do.

I do that. Polite to a fault is my motto. Polite to customers, polite to the grocery store clerks and post office workers. Even when they are not polite in return. It is easy with practice.

Our first customer of the day is a high school-age kid, probably cutting class. I take in the dyed black hair and black clothes and predict his trajectory and sure enough, he beelines for the horror shelves. He tries to ignore me, but I make sure to greet him properly and sunnily. The surly teen looks about ready to hiss back but pauses and nods instead. Aha, the power of good manners strikes again.

From then on, the day progresses as per usual. At noon, Tim brings the mail. Mr. B sorts through it, then orders lunch from the deli across the street. We eat our sandwiches and crunch on the delicious homemade pickles, the deli's specialty. Mr. B drinks Strawberry Yoo-hoo, one of his only indulgences, while I stick with water.

"Mmm." He hums his pleasure and smacks his lips to further the point.

"I haven't had one of those since I was a kid. In fact, I've never seen an adult drink them," I told him the first time we shared a meal.

"99% fat-free, caffeine-free, loaded with calcium and Vitamin D. So much to love." Mr. B holds up the bottle Vanna

White style.

"You can practically do their ads."

"Just what they need, an old fogey pimping their berry juice."

I laugh. Then I gather our trash, dispose of it, and get ready to go to the post office. We do some online business. Mr. B was reluctant at first, but it's too practical not to, and so easy.

The post office is about a ten-minute bike ride. I love biking. It's one of those childhood things you can do at any age and enjoy and not look silly while at it. Mr. B gave me his old bike, now that he can't ride it. It's a battered but mechanically sound Schwinn that's probably close to me in age and once upon a time used to be red. It has a rear rack with a set of metal panniers attached to it and a front basket, so I can do all of our errands on it. Which is great, because my driver's license lapsed ages ago, and I'm not even sure I remember how to drive anymore or would be comfortable doing it.

This way I can get haul our packages to the post office and haul the groceries home. It's a great setup, a great set of wheels. Portable independence, really.

Mr. B has a car, or used to at any rate, though I've not seen him drive in ages. He has a deal with the local garage where he keeps it, safe and sound, away from the elements.

I know the route to the post office by heart, can probably do it with my eyes closed. Today, though, since my eyes are open, I spy something out of the corner of one. Don't know what, a slight movement, a figure? I'm not sure, but the distraction is enough to send me off course and to the pavement.

Not a terrible fall by any means, the only things injured are my head and my pride. The packaged books, I'm relieved to notice, are safe and sound. The Schwinn's good too. I remount and pedal away, hoping no one saw that embarrassing display of cycling ineptitude.

The post office people know me by name but mostly refer to me as The Book Guy or Books, for short. I know them by name too, it's the polite thing to do.

"Hey, Books, how's it hanging?"

"Hey, Terry. All good here. Got five packages today to ship out. How are you?"

"Oh man, don't ask. My mother-in-law is coming to stay for a week. Can I crash at your place?"

"Would if I could, Terry," I tell him and smile. I don't know if anyone knows about my living situation. I certainly never mention it. In fact, I remember Terry from when he was a letter carrier and I was on the streets, before we both graduated to our much cushier positions in life. He never noticed me then and never made the connection later. It's good, reminds me of how tangible the changes I've made are.

The packages are going to Ohio, New York, Pennsylvania, Oregon, and California. All over. The books we sell travel much further than I ever did. I was never very adventurous and, outside of the quotidian summer trips to the beach, neither were my grandparents. My parents died when I was young. My grandparents raised me, but they were old when they started and older still when they were done. The cemetery they're buried in is quite lovely and peaceful. I visit them from time to time. Back in the day, I've even slept there on occasion. The night security was lax to nonexistent. Not much to steal and, I guess, they took a chance with the vandals.

After some more small talk with Terry, I head back. We don't need any groceries just now; I went shopping only a couple of days ago. Strangely enough, I enjoy grocery shopping. I don't think many people do, the way they look all harried and put out at the store, torn between their phones and their kids and their other plans. For me, it's peaceful and homey, and reminds me of the most pleasing aspects of normal life: nourishment, meal planning, etc. I read the circulars thoroughly and make sure to take advantage of the deals. I try new things at the sample stations. Sometimes I treat us to some new and exciting product, something from the bakery, usually.

Money isn't an object, it seems, or at least Mr. B has never complained about how much I spend, though I always make sure to provide him with a receipt and highlight the savings. I don't want to be seen as taking advantage. I owe him too much.

Besides giving me a place to live and a job I love, he also pays me a small salary. It's in cash, and I hide it in an old cookie box at the bottom of one of the crates in my room. No idea what to do with it or what to spend it on as of yet, but I love the option.

I've tried making plans for my future, but it never sticks. It never even materializes fully. I think plans are for other people, people who haven't hit the bottom of the barrel of life and waited there desperately trying to climb out or be rescued. I'm just so happy to be where I am, to have what I have, that to want something besides it—to even contemplate that want—seems borderline sacrilegious. I'm content to be content and perpetuate in my comfortable existence as long as I may be permitted to do so. I've conveyed as much to Mr. B when he asked me about it, and he seems to get it.

I think Mr. B understands second acts because he's living in one of his own. He doesn't talk much about his life before the bookstore. But from what he's let drop over the years, I've gathered that he was never married and had no kids, that he worked some white-collar desk job in an office, I believe in accounting, and that after a life of careful saving and smart financial planning, he was able to retire to a childhood dream of his and buy this bookstore.

Sounds nice, doesn't it?

I always think there must be more to it, more to him. Sometimes I think I notice secrets twinkle in his eyes. Sometimes I think there's a double meaning to what he says or some double entendre to a joke he makes, but I've never been too great with such subtleties and, after the life I've had, I know not to pry. People are entitled to their secrets, entitled to the compartmentalization of their past. Otherwise, the weight of accumulated years and experiences might prove too heavy to lug around. Live and let live, there's a motto to go by. Live and let live.

When I get back to the store, there's a lull. Looks like I'm winning today's bet. There's no prize, of course. I'd be happier selling more books any day.

I check the internet sales instead. That's my job, maintaining our online presence. Mr. B says he's too old-fashioned for all that. Me, I love the internet. Love having an entire world at my fingertips. Granted, I don't understand some aspects of it, and I positively loathe some others. Don't even get me started on social media for socializing's sake. The trends, the apps, the trolls in the comment sections … at best bewilders and at worst terrifies me. But I love all the information, the ease of access to it. The documentary videos, the science articles, book reviews. I can get lost online and spend happy hours there. And so, I do, after updating our pages, answering some questions from potential buyers, and noting books to pack and ship for the next day.

I drop an hour at *Atlas Obscura* alone, dreaming faraway dreams. Then I check my usual haunts, *NatGeo*, *Popular Science*, etc.

I barely notice when it gets dark outside. Soon enough the closing time is upon us. I did win, it was a slow day after all. The most eventful thing to happen all day was me hitting my head on some shelves. I'm still not sure how it happened, I was straightening out the occult section, which is a pretty generous description for a two-shelf setup, and next thing I knew I was on the floor. A heavy book out of place might have done it, or maybe I just misjudged the distance or got distracted. I'm taller than I think I am. It was nothing really, not even a proper goose egg to show for it. That's two head traumas in one day, though. I hope I don't have a concussion. I chastise myself for carelessness.

"It'll pick up tomorrow," I say like I always do.

Mr. B nods. He's tired and wants to be off his feet, says his recliner at home is calling his name. He goes up. I lock up, clean up.

Supper is a quick and easy affair of mac'n'cheese prepared on a hotplate in my room. I finish and wash up for the night. Get back to bed to read myself to sleep.

I'm stepping away from Christopher Moore right now with this new book. It's a good one, this latest thriller from an author I had recently discovered through a customer. I'm usually good at figuring out the plot twists, but I'm about four-fifths of the way in and still have no idea. I fall asleep before I finish, exhaustion overriding suspense.

I don't know what wakes me up in the middle of the night, but something does. Something that sounds distinctly like a woman's voice.

Nothing wakes you up like fear. Your heart can go zero to sixty in car metaphors, and stay there, dispelling all the comforts of slumber instantaneously. And fear is a funny thing because it doesn't deal in absolutes. It's contingent upon so many factors, and time of day seems to be the main one of them. Which is to say, all things are scarier at night. All thoughts, all sounds.

A female voice isn't scary in and of itself. It's something one hears on a daily basis. A female voice in a locked store, in your room, in the middle of the night is another story altogether.

I sit up and say "Hello" immediately cringing inwardly. It's the stupidest thing to say in this sort of situation. Why would you ever greet a possible intruder, announce your presence, or give away your location? I've always thought the characters who did it in books and movies were idiots, and here I am … being that idiot.

"Hello," she says.

I want to turn on my lamp, but I can't move my arms. I seem to be literally paralyzed by fear. I didn't know that was a real thing. She doesn't sound scary, she sounds … lost, and young.

"Don't be afraid."

Easy for her to say. I don't want to be afraid; I shouldn't

be. I've seen things, terrible, terrible things, in my time. During my first stay in the mental institution—a state-operated and underfunded horror show of a place—I saw a man set himself on fire. I didn't know him, didn't know what caused him to do that. All I remember is screaming all around him, and his face—he was smiling a strangely knowing smile like he knew just what he was doing, and it was the only way, like he pitied those who weren't in the know. That smile haunted my nightmares for years.

I find my voice. "Who are you?"

"I'm an angel," comes the reply.

"Is there such a thing?"

"Of course."

"What would I see if I turned on the light?"

"I'm not sure," she says sadly.

"Why not?"

"Because I've been visiting you for so long, and this is

the first time you've heard me."

This is getting weirder and weirder. "You've been here before?"

"Jared," she says, "I never left."

That sends an icicle down my spine. I don't have to have this conversation. I don't have to engage. I'm having a relapse of some sort, a chemical flashback my addled brain is putting on. Maybe I hit my head too hard on those shelves after all. Maybe I'm going crazy or returning to crazy. Either way, I don't have to engage. She isn't real.

"You're not real," I tell her.

"I know," she replies.

"Will you go away, please?" I whisper.

"I will if you help me."

"What do you want help with?"

"I want justice."

"For what?"

"I'll tell you when you're ready."

"I'm ready now."

"You're not."

She's right, of course. I'm not ready. For whatever it is. For whatever this is.

"Are you really an angel?"

"Are you really a man?" she counters.

"I once knew a man who said he talked to angels. By the time they were through with him, he was nothing but a drooling mess on the floor."

"You are not going mad, if that's what you're thinking."

"Oh, no?" I throw my hands in the air, exasperatedly. "This is all just perfectly normal?"

"I haven't known normal in a very long time." She sounds sad again.

"Well, I can tell you, it isn't this. People don't talk to angels in the middle of the night."

"Of course they do." It sounds like she smiles." Haven't you ever heard of religion?"

"Not like this," I tell her, shaking my head. "Not like this."

"What would you prefer?"

"I would prefer to have remained asleep. I would prefer for this conversation to not have happened at all."

She doesn't respond. I hear quiet whispering, it's as if she's talking to someone else. I wait.

"I'm sorry," she says, eventually. "I'm sorry it has to be this way. It isn't fair to you".

"Were you talking to someone just now?"

"Don't you think you have enough to process already?"

"Are there ..." The notion is too frightening to contemplate, but I ask anyway. "Are there more of you?'

"Jared," she says impatiently but not unkindly, "concentrate on me."

"OK." *No, not okay, not okay at all.*

"I don't want you to worry ..." *Well, that ship has sailed.* "Or be afraid" *Ditto.* "You're not going crazy." *Debatable.* "And I mean you no harm." *Should have led with that probably, no?* "We ... I just need your help."

Strangely enough, I believe her or want to. She sounds sincere, she sounds sad, but above all, she sounds sane. Perfectly sane. Which means the crazy one here must be ...

And with that disturbing thought, I finally regain control over my limbs. I reach out and turn on the light beside my bed. I don't know what I expected to see, but there's no one there, I'm all alone.

"Angel?" I whisper tentatively, looking around as if this might just be some elaborate hide and seek game.

Nothing. Silence. No one here in this room but me, nothing here but my meager possessions.

I try telling myself it didn't happen, couldn't have. Like the most anti-climactic and unimaginative of all fictional endings: *and then he woke up and realized it was all but a dream*. But in my heart of hearts I know, I *know* she was here. I know we spoke. I know she'll be back.

It's these thoughts, these frightening terrible thoughts, that make sure I stay awake the rest of the night, pricking up my ears, peering into the darkness. Waiting.

People have always needed stories. When the first humans to walk the Earth gathered around the fire after a long day and looked up at the inexplicable star-dotted skies above them, dwarfed by the darkness, in desperate need of something to take their mind off it or maybe even to explain the mysterious world around them, they'd turn to each other and say, "Tell me a story." Whatever that sounded like in prehistoric grunts.

Slowly that desire, that need, has transformed itself into books. Where there are books, there are booksellers, and so it goes. We are a crucial strand in the fabric of society.

That was the gist of one of the first things Mr. B ever told me. He likes to get philosophical in the mornings, says it counteracts the news-induced ennui and depression. And so he goes on these tangents, sometimes morality lectures, but more often historical facts pertaining directly to books and bookselling. The things the man knows.

I love listening to him. I'm a good listener. Given a choice, I'd always rather listen than talk. Less to think about, less to worry about that way.

And this morning I have a lot to worry about.

I get through our customary breakfast quieter than ever. My thoughts are racing. I can't wait to get online, but at the same time, I'm afraid of what my research will show me.

A large donation comes in and takes my mind of my mind for a while. I carry the heavy boxes to the side, where we have a table set up just to process those. I could have used a dolly, but it's so unwieldy that it's almost always easier to just shoulder the weight.

Six large cardboard boxes. Every one of them a mystery. You never know what you're going to find. Statistically speaking, most of the donations are trash, moldy volumes unearthed from someone's basement, beat-up mass-market paperbacks, old copies of *Readers' Digests* … well, you get the idea. But every so often, there's a treasure. Mr. B taught me to look for those, and it's fun now that I've mastered it.

This isn't an outright waste of time; I can tell straight away. There's no tell-tale malodor, nothing like that. These are well-kept books. Someone loved these books, collected them, delighted in them.

A mix of hardbacks and trade paperbacks, a variety of subjects, mostly scholarly—history, archeology, biographies—with a dash of classics and noir detective stories. We can work with that.

I sort the books into categories, arrange them by condition, look for first editions, collectibles, signed copies, etc. Mr. B is at the front desk, talking to the guy who brought the books in. I overhear snippets of the conversation … father died … collected for years … no credit necessary (guess the son isn't a reader) … donation receipt … thank you.

The guy leaves and Mr. B makes his way over.

"Anything?" he asks me.

"Yeah, these are good. No treasures yet, but I'm not finished."

Mr. B browses the piles I've created. "An academic type, huh?"

"Looks like it."

The bell above the entrance rings, announcing a customer.

"Well, I'll leave you to it, old sport."

I clock the Gatsby reference with small satisfaction. It was one of the first books Mr. B had me read. I don't know how I managed to avoid that book my entire life. Don't know why I did, don't know why anyone would. It quickly became one of my favorites, and even now that I have read so many others, it remains the top five of all time, easily.

Something about a guy who does whatever it takes, follows the American dream to a tee, and gets burned by it, just rings true to me.

I was never a Gatsby, of course, I'm more of a Nick, happy to observe from the sidelines.

I get to the last box and—surprise, surprise—a change of pace. The last box is all true crime. A popular genre, for sure, made all the more so by the recent string of TV serial documentaries on various famous killers, but it seems incongruous by comparison to the rest of the collection.

These books are of a recent and well-thumbed variety. Guess it takes all types. Personally, I never understood the obsession, but it's definitely a thing, even if going by store sales alone.

I know one thing—Larry will be thrilled. Larry lives for true crime. He comes in once or twice a week and heads straight for that aisle. His manners leave something to be desired, and his appearance can be at best described as a child molester from the eighties. I know it isn't charitable, but you look at his shiny bald pate ringed with a tight half-donut of black hair, his tinted large plastic frame glasses hiding his too close-together eyes, his weird too-large mustache, and tell me otherwise.

Mr. B is all about judge not lest you be judged approach to customers, so I try. I tried with Larry for a long time before he started actually talking to me. Now I can't shut him up. But he is a good customer, and so I end up listening to the tales of his macabre obsession.

Larry is short, 5'6" at most, and generally potato-shaped. I've yet to hear him tell a joke that's as funny as he thinks it is. And I'm not crazy about the way he looks at female customers when he thinks he's being subtle. I don't think he's dangerous or anything, more of a garden-variety creep. He teaches driving for a living. For all I know he is a perfectly nice man, but I wouldn't put my kids in a car with him. Just saying.

I'll have to give him a call now, though. He lives for this. He specifically left his phone number at the store for when collections like these come in.

I finish cataloging the books, then take the selected few over to my computer station to check their resale value. Until now I've managed to usefully put the events of last night out of my mind. But now the world wide web is before me, and the thoughts come flooding back.

I type in "adult schizophrenia onset." I type in "LSD lingering results." I type in "acid flashbacks.". I read and I read and I read. There's so much information out there to weed through. And so much of it is inconclusive. I can't get a yes or no, just statistics. Okay, I'll play the odds.

Odds are I'm not schizophrenic, as that usually happens earlier in adulthood. Odds are I may not be crazy at all. I may simply have night terrors or be a very vivid dreamer. Odds are

…

I need to stop. I stop. I have things to do. I can't be spinning out like that. Mr. B is counting on me. And the truth of it is, in the bright light of day—or the version of it that comes into the bookstore—it does seem like a nightmare.

Something not quite real enough, not as real as the night's darkness rendered it.

And so, I set all that aside and proceed to look up the books, find a few worth listing online and do so. Call Larry and leave him a voicemail. Have lunch with Mr. B. Assist some customers.

Evening comes before I know it. We lock up. Mr. B wishes me good night. Tells me he hopes I'll finish the thriller tonight so we can discuss the twist in the morning. I promise him I will. I sincerely hope it'll be the only twist my night will hold.

Back in my room, I make beans on toast. A weird dish I got out of books and learned to like. Easy, tasty, quick. I read until I start dozing off. Get up, use the bathroom, do some stretches to wake up, then read some more. The twist is a killer one. No pun intended.

I fall asleep shortly after I finish the book, hoping for an uneventful slumber.

"Jared."

"Jared."

I'm not hearing that, I'm not … I pull the pillow over my head. "Go away," I mumble sleepily.

"Jared," the voice insists.

Well, shitbiscuits, now I'm up. I rub the sleep from my eyes. The voice's owner is still nowhere to be found, but she will not be denied.

"You're back," I say ruefully.

"You're not happy about it."

"Well observed, Sherlock."

"I told you I needed your help, I …"

"Look," I interrupt her. "What are you? Who are you? Can you tell me at least that much? Am I going crazy?"

"Do you think you're going crazy?"

She sounds just like this one shrink I use to see. I hated that guy.

"I just need to know this …" I steady myself. "… before I can contemplate helping you."

"I told you already—I'm an angel. All of us are."

"An angel?"

"It's what he would call us, it's what he made us."

"He?"

"You wouldn't believe me if I told you."

"Try me." I cringe inwardly, preparing for a sermon.

She sounds like she's talking quietly, but not to me.

"Who are you talking to?"

"The other angels." *Oh right, of course.*

"How many of you are there?"

"Seventeen."

"Why that number?"

"He never told us."

"Okay … Why can't I see you?"

"Because you don't believe."

"Good one, Santa."

"You sound angry. Or maybe upset. We don't want you to be angry or upset."

That I believe. But who wouldn't be angry or upset under the circumstances?

"So, make me believe in you."

"It doesn't work like that," she says sadly.

"What doesn't?"

"Faith."

Back to that, okay. "Is this a religious thing?"

"No, not at all. At least two of us think it would help if you were a believer, but all you need is a good heart."

"How do I know if my heart is good? How would you?"

"We've been watching you. We think you're our best bet."

"Why not Mr. B?"

There's a sudden pall in the room. A palpable silence.

"He is not a good man," the voice says after a while.

"Oh, yes he is." I may not know this about myself, but I

know this about him, for a fact. "He saved me, saved my life. He is smart and he is kind and ..."

Suddenly there's a whoosh, like a cyclone of voices all talking at once, talking over each other, gaining a physical momentum, enough of one to knock over the book and the lamp from my makeshift nightstand.

This is new. This is new and scary.

"Okay." I hold up my hands, "Okay, so you don't like Mr. B, and I'm your designated knight in shining armor. What can I do for you? Talk to me. Tell me your story."

There's only silence.

"Angel?" I whisper tentatively into it. "Are you still there?"

No, of course not. She's gone now, if she was ever even there to begin with. I'm all alone and there's suddenly nothing comforting about my comfortable bed in my comfortable room. A poison was left behind to work on me and now I can't sleep.

"Once upon a time, a man named Vespasiano da Bisticci, a well-known Florence bookseller and manuscript dealer, became so outraged that books would no longer be written out by hand that he closed his shop in a fit of rage and became the first person in history to prophesize the death of the book industry."

That seems to be the bookseller history lesson of the day. Mr. B holds up the book he's reading, cover out, so I can see what it is: *The Bookshop Book* by Jen Campbell.

Mr. B goes on to explain that Vespasiano was technically the first publisher and commercial bookseller (this is according to Basbanes's *Gentle Madness*) and that he mass-produced books for Cosimo de Medici in the mid-1400s and helped Pope Nicholas V assemble the Vatican's manuscript collection. All the books he sold, though, "had to be written with the pen," he said years later, as "anything else would have made the collector feel ashamed."

"And yet the book business persevered and, despite all the naysayers, here we are."

"Here we are." I nod, saluting him with my coffee.

"You look tired, Kemosabe," he says, peering at me closely.

I rub my eyes. I know they've got dark bags under them, I can practically feel it.

"Nightmares."

"Any fun ones?"

"Nah." I shake my head. The Pop-Tart this morning tastes like cardboard. I check the flavor: it's strawberry, my favorite. I *am* out of it.

"We can interpret those for you. I'm sure we've got a book on dreams somewhere around here," Mr. B offers amiably.

"What's it say about angels, you think?" I ask.

He gives me a funny look. I can't blame him.

"You're not going religious on me, are you?"

"No, I…no, just weird dreams. Forget about it. I'm trying to."

"Well, okay then. What's on your docket for the day?"

"Post office, for sure. Bios needs some straightening out too, I noticed. And Larry said he was stopping by."

"Oh, good. That's always good for business."

I nod, midway through my apple.

"So long as it isn't my ear he's chewing off," Mr. B adds jocularly.

"Last time he went on this crazy rant about the new Bundy movie."

"Didn't see it."

"Me neither. And now I don't have too. Larry pretty much did a scene by scene for me. Apparently, it was a very sympathetic representation."

"He was a charismatic guy, by all accounts."

"So they say. Guess it's unavoidable in this day and age—everyone's so fascinated with serial killers, they make them seem more likable. Because if they weren't at all likeable, if they were just outright monstrous, then what would it say about people's obsessions with them?"

"That's pretty insightful, Kemosabe." Mr. B looks at me with a difficult-to-interpret expression. Interest? Pride? He takes off his glasses and cleans them meticulously with a neat, monogrammed handkerchief, the only man I've ever met who carries one. Without the protective shield of curved lens, his eyes look different, younger, sharper. And then the glasses are back on, and he looks just the same.

"If you get tired today, feel free to go take a nap. Don't want you falling over in the aisles," he tells me.

"Thanks." I nod and rub my hands together. "But I'll be alright once I start moving. Already feel the caffeine kicking in."

"Okay, then."

Annie comes in. She's a flight attendant—I believe that's the correct nomenclature these days—and has the personality to match: bright, sparky, eternally upbeat. Annie prefers paper books for her flights, because she's always losing them, and they are cheaper to replace than Kindles.

"What's good, Jared?"

"Books are," I answer as always. It's kind of our thing.

In a different world I would consider the possibility of Annie flirting with me, in a very different world I'd even consider the possibility of flirting back. In this world I'm a realist with a past as beat-up and checkered as a cheap tablecloth at a cheap diner. I know I wouldn't stand a chance and don't intend to embarrass myself—and her—trying.

I was in love once. I thought I was, anyway. She, like me, was sectioned for a suicide attempt; that's where we met. How's that for modern romance?

The thing is, I shouldn't have been there in the first place. I wasn't trying, it was just a mistake, a misunderstanding. Cherry (yeah, her mom really did that to her) was caught dead to rights, (forgive the pun, she loved puns), bleeding out in the bathtub from her (correctly, vertically) slashed wrists by her roommate who came home earlier than she was supposed to.

Do you know how this story ends? Not happily. We had fun for a while, but ultimately, nothing I could offer her beat out the promise of the eternal rest she imagined. She tried again and that time succeeded.

I know it's unfashionable these days to say someone committed suicide, but the thing is, all that political correctness aside, Cherry did commit suicide. She decided on it, planned it, and carried it out. That's commitment. To override our most basic human instinct—the need for self-preservation— and do something like that … well, that's a deliberate, chosen action. A wrong action, of course, but still it took agency and deliberation. I'm not about to take that away from her.

She had her reasons, it isn't up to me or anyone else to validate them. It was her screwed up brain, sure, but it was her life. She did with it as she wanted. Took control of what she could. I regret what she did every day, but I learned to respect her choice and live with it. I also learned never to get that close to anyone ever again.

And so, I banter with Annie to the best of my abilities. I laugh at her jokes. I make book recommendations. But I don't accept her casual invites to hang out, I don't reciprocate her casual body contact gestures, and we don't go get coffee. It's best that way, for everyone.

Annie leaves with the latest thriller by an overrated British author, the sort of easy breezy beach read Reese Witherspoon would rave about. I head out to the post office.

Terry's full of complaints about his mother-in-law. I

sympathize, ship, and leave.

I stop by the grocery store on the way back and take my time shopping, pushing the cart around when I could have done with a basket, checking out what others are doing and buying, trying some samples. I get back to the bookstore just in time for lunch.

"That Annie girl seems to like you."

"She's just friendly."

"Don't you want a nice friend like Annie?"

I try to make some sort of a joke about how I'd never date a customer so as to not jeopardize our sales in case it didn't work out.

Mr. B pretends to be amused, then asks me seriously, "You don't get lonely, kid?"

"No." I shake my head. "I honestly don't." It's true too. Loneliness is a matter of perspective. Some people say that about happiness, which I don't buy, but for loneliness I think it actually applies. You adjust your expectations sufficiently, and voila, you're okay.

Life isn't a rom-com or a great love story, it isn't defined by romantic entanglements, at least it doesn't have to be. I'm content with my lot in life, I really am.

"What about you, Mr. B?" I ask, uncharacteristically veering into dangerously personal territory.

"Oh, I've had my fun in the sun." He smiles wistfully. "Now in the autumn of my days, I'm quite happy as I am."

I nod, pleased he's happy. Pleased we're on the same page. Pleased nothing has to change.

Larry doesn't come in, after all. He calls to say he's got a last-minute lesson with a kid who was freaking out about the driving exam tomorrow, and he couldn't say no. Larry begs me to hold on to the stock for an extra day, and I reassure him that it's no problem. True crime's popular enough, but those books don't zoom off the shelves the way he must imagine they do.

Eventually, we close the shop. Mr. B wins the daily totals. I retire to my room and watch a profoundly disturbing documentary about former Nazis who went on to flee prosecution, settle abroad, and live perfectly normal lives. It boggles the mind how people notorious for such atrocities could just go on to have a perfectly normal second act in life, suspected by no one. How does someone compartmentalize themselves like that? Or did they really change? Did extraordinary circumstances like war make them into a certain type of people, and then ordinary circumstances like peace made them into another type? Does it work like that? I don't know enough about psychology to figure this out. I resolve to discuss this with Mr. B.

Sleep comes and takes me away. It is, at last, dreamless.

Upon waking, perfectly rested, I feel as if the two previous angelic visitations must have been nothing but dreams, after all, or possibly the aftermath of a slight concussion. I go through my morning stretches and ablutions a happy man, happy and refreshed, someone whose life makes sense. Ah, lovely.

The next morning, the sun is shining brightly, the day is unseasonably warm. I'm halfway through a chocolate Pop-Tart and almost all the way through telling Mr. B about the documentary I watched.

"Hmm," he says, stroking his beard. I think most people who grow out beards do it just for the opportunity to do that. Or maybe I'm just jealous. I couldn't grow a beard if I tried, I don't even need to shave that often. I'd probably have one of those babyfaces if it wasn't so good at reflecting the wear and tear of the years past. As it is, between the naturally youthful looks and the toll of the life I've led, I average out to look about my age. There's even some grey in the temples that's starting to come in.

"So, what do you think about it?" I ask.

"About what?"

"You know, second chances."

"I guess I believe in those."

"Without reservations?"

"Like a cheap diner." He smiles. I smile back but persist.

"Even for criminals? Even for murderers?"

"Well, are we talking justice or are we talking second chances here? Because the former is dished out by society, and the latter is done to an individual. Society throughout history has had some really peculiar ideas about justice. Just check out how recently there were laws on the books regarding punishing homosexuality or even witches. There are some places in the world where stoning is still a thing. So, it's all punitive, not redemptional in intent. You do something society disapproves of, and it punishes you for it. End of story. No second chances. Or a person who did all these socially deemed "terrible" things can just stop, maybe even atone, and change his ways of his own accord. That's entirely different. The end result is the same—no more crime, by whatever definition. But the public's bloodthirst isn't satisfied that way. And people are bloodthirsty. Not that long ago, watching someone hang was like going to the movies. Gladiator games to the death were one of the greatest spectacles ever put on. So, what you're asking me is, do people need to be punished for their crimes? And what I'm telling you is that society isn't rigged up to dish out justice, not proper condign justice, just an arbitrary sort based on modern and malleable sensibilities. I believe that a person can punish himself for their own sins if they choose to do so, can improve himself. Guess you can say I believe in the power of an individual, a triumph of one's will over one's baser instincts and so on."

Wow. I'm taken aback, Pop-Tart forgotten on my plate. That's the most Mr. B has ever expounded on any one subject outside of books and book business. I make a mental note to look up the definition for condign too. Otherwise, I don't know what to say.

"That was a lot, wasn't it?"

I nod. "Interesting, though. Definitely food for thought."

"Sorry, kiddo. Guess I'm just full of piss and vinegar and strong opinions this morning." He smiles into his beard. "Anyway, what's on your docket for the day? Can you squeeze in a grocery run?"

"Sure."

But first things first, inventory and shelving of new thriller stock. Probably our most popular genre. After a while, all the books are starting to look the same. There's a woman on the cover, a title featuring the word woman or girl or wife. Usually, a female author too. The plot summaries don't show that much variation either. But hey, people are eating those up.

Annie pops to mind with her latest selection. The perennially perky Annie and her easy charm. I shake the thought out of my head. Concentrate on the task at hand.

At lunchtime, Larry comes in. I show him to the pile of books I've saved for him, putting off eating my sandwich until later.

Mr. B can't stand Larry, probably the only customer he can't stand. He appreciates his business but avoids dealing with him directly whenever possible. I don't mind, I'm used to him.

Larry's baldness is shining with sweat. He really needs to get into the handkerchief-carrying thing.

"Hot enough for ya?" he says by the way of greeting. Then repeats it, wiping his forehead with the back of his hand.

I think it might be his idea of humor, the way he tends to say obvious things in repetition. I smile politely.

"I've been waiting to check out these books. Been really looking forward to it." His voice modulates itself weirdly but mostly stays on the quiet side, with a whiny undertone.

"Well, here they are."

He browses, his eyes light up. I hope there are other things in his life that make his eyes light up the way books about murders and murderers do. But then again, I don't want to know.

"This is a classic." He holds one up. "You ever read it?"

"I've heard of it," I prevaricate.

Larry launches into the summary. It sounds disturbingly similar to a lot of true crime books he has talked to me about over the time I've known him.

"Terrible business," I say when he finishes.

"Isn't it, though," he agrees, but his tone says we're nowhere near the same page on this.

He sets a few more books aside and then grows still with something like reverence.

"Oh," he says, lightly placing his fingers on the hardcover tome before him. "Would you look at that."

I look. It's got some sort of a crude effigy of an angel on the cover, an author's name I've never heard of. The title is …

"The Angelmaker." Larry practically breathes it out, hushed by awe. "You know how long I've been looking for this?"

I wait for him to tell me.

"This book is pretty much impossible to find. And a first edition." He turns it this way and that in his hands. His hands, I notice, are sweating.

"You've made my day, kid." He beams at me.

I don't like when he calls me that. I don't like when anyone but Mr. B calls me that. Frankly, I'm pretty sure Larry isn't old enough to call me that, but I can never tell. He's got one of those faces like he was never really young to begin with. He could be in his late thirties or fifties, and I'd never guess.

Larry puts the book down on his to-buy pile and wipes his hands on his dad-cut jeans. Those, a sweatshirt, and a cheap-looking, sturdy pair of slip-on shoes usually complete his outfit. Clean and mostly odor-free despite the profuse sweating, but the man is not a sharp dresser by any means.

"You know about this guy?"

I shake my head no.

"You should. He's a local. Or was a local. Never caught, so we'll never know. But he reigned terror on these streets decades ago. And then just stopped."

Okay, this is kind of interesting, actually. I'll listen. I don't need to spur Larry on, he's happy to expound.

"So, this guy, right, this guy, he musta been obsessed with angels. This was back in the eighties. Young girls or young women or whatever you're supposed to say, they started disappearing. In numbers that you couldn't just explain with runaways and other stupid things young people do. In their places, there'd be an effigy of an angel left. Hence the name, right? Right? OK, so they investigated and found nothing. Each crime scene was as clean as the proverbial whistle. The uncertainty was brutal, it's kinda what drove everyone crazy. See, the thing with serial killers is that they need to be caught. Caught, put away, and explained. That way the world can move on. Right? But this guy, there was no catching him. There was no evidence. And worst of all and most important of all, there were no bodies. So, in the end, nothing could be done. And then one day he just stopped, and that was that."

"He just got away with it?" I can't help it, I am intrigued.

"Well, yeah, if these girls were indeed taken and murdered, then he did. He totally did. And this was brutal, you understand, because all the families of these girls never got any sort of closure. They were just stuck in a sort of limbo, while the guy himself became a local legend. The boogeyman. And then one day, a few years later, a series of letters arrived at the local newspaper confessing the crimes. Anonymous. Anonymous, of course. This guy claimed to have taken the girls but said he was done, it was all done and over with now, and never again. And sure enough, never again."

"And they never found him?"

"No, the letters were as clean as his crime scenes. No prints, no hints. He got away with it. The Angelmaker, that's what the papers christened him. And it stuck. Our very own local mystery."

Larry pauses, looks at me expectantly, wanting me to be as bewildered and awed by this as he seems to be. I don't think he finds what he's looking for, but he goes on anyway.

"You see, that's the best thing a serial killer can possibly ever do. Leave a mystery like that. You know how many serial killers there have been? Tons. Tons most people have never even heard of. And yet everyone in the world has heard of Jack the Ripper. Not because his body count was crazy high, not cause he was the most brutal or most original, but because he was never caught. Nothing makes an impression like a proper mystery. The Zodiac killer came close, but there were bodies there. This guy … nothing, not a trace."

Larry's eyes are glowing with something disturbingly close to admiration. Me, I'm just disturbed. And surprised to never have heard about this until now. Guess that disproves Larry's theory, in a way. Granted, I've spent a lot of my time drifting as far away from this world as I could manage, but still … I wonder how many people these days remember the serial killer that Larry can't forget.

Something's nagging me about this entire thing, though. "So, why did he send the letters, then?"

"Aha, good question. Very good question. The popular theory is that he must have reformed or something, maybe found religion, or was on his deathbed, and decided to confess his sins and unload his soul. Provide some closure for those poor families. Kinda noble if you ask me."

I wouldn't, Larry, I wouldn't.

"Well, anyway, gotta go. Got a lesson at one. Nice chatting with you, kid. I'll take all of these."

"Right, sure, Larry. Let me bring them up front and ring them up for you."

After Larry leaves, I think about the story he told me. I can't stop thinking about it. All day, throughout my errands, it haunts my mind. What sort of a person would do something like that? What sort of a person was this Angelmaker?

I ask Mr. B if he's ever heard about the case.

"Well, sure, I've heard of it, it was impossible not to in the eighties," he tells me as his face darkens. "You really shouldn't talk to Larry so much. You don't want any more nightmares."

He's right, of course, but I can't help thinking about it even as I go to bed. My nightmares seldom seem to have much to do with my daily life anyway. I figure it's safe. Plus, I've already been dreaming of angels, so …

Every so often Mr. B gives me an afternoon off. He used to try to make it an entire day, but we both quickly realized that's entirely too much free time for me. I don't want it, I prefer to stay busy, idle hands and all that.

So, now it's down to an occasional afternoon. I seldom do much with this free time. Sometimes I take in a movie. Most of the time I just take my lunch and a book and go to the park. It's a nice park. The town had gone all out cleaning up a once-abandoned lot at the insistence of a neighborhood coalition. There are comfortable benches beneath well taken care of trees. There's a large playground for the kiddies. A statue of a local war hero-slash-long-time beloved mayor. There's even a fountain with a layer of shiny coins at the bottom, signifying the wishes, hopes, and dreams of the visitors.

I have a favorite bench. I like to people-watch. It's a guilty pleasure, of sorts. I never want to engage with them, join in their games, share in their fun. I just like to watch from the sidelines. There's something very comforting about the quotidian rhythms of the lives of others. The way I figure it, I've had my fun, overdid it, and now I'm done with it. My fun now is a good book, a cup of warm cocoa, a decent historical documentary, and, of course, the bookstore.

I'm thinking about the bookstore right now during my off time. Mr. B would not approve. Then again, he was the one who told me that life/work balance is a myth that modern American society has steadily done away with. "The exigencies of Mammon," as he puts it. The best-case scenario is finding a job you love, so that it doesn't feel like work. Well, we got that going for us.

I'm finishing up my latest Christopher Moore romp, a perfect read for a sunny day. I brought a sandwich, an apple, and a liter bottle of water with me. I'm good for hours.

Sometimes I pause my reading, look up, and take in the world around me. I watch the fit people in the latest athleisure fashions jog, stretch, walk. I should really do something like that, but I can never find the motivation. I'm skinny and likely to remain that way—I think my early years of fun had done a number on my metabolism—but probably not as fit as they are. I'm strong enough from hauling book boxes, but that doesn't give you gym muscles. I don't own a single piece of athleisure unless you count an old pair of lounging sweats I sleep in when the weather drops.

I overhear snippets of conversations. Sometimes it takes a second to realize they are directed to the people who aren't there. Headphone tech is getting smaller and smaller and wireless now too. Used to be, you saw someone standing alone and talking, you'd know they were talking to themselves and know to avoid them. These days you can barely tell. And everyone, *everyone*, is buried in their phones.

You'd think they'd look up, take in the nature, notice the

world, but they seldom do. And when they do, it's to take a photo of it. We live in the most photographed and least experienced time. I go back to my book; the world starts to fade away.

"Jared."

I look up. *Oh, crap.*

"Jared, I hardly recognized you outside of the bookstore."

"Hi, Larry."

"I've been meaning to come by and talk to you, actually, so I'm glad I saw you."

"What's up?" I suppress a sigh and close the book upon a bookmark. It's the one from our store, store logo and all. I love that owl.

"It's about the book I bought from you the other day."

The other day? It's been a week, at least, I think. Sleeping without nightmares this entire time has done wonders for my disposition and confused my sense of time.

"Something wrong with the book, Larry? You know we don't do refunds, but I'd be happy to arrange a store credit for you."

"No, no, it's nothing like that." He wipes his shiny sweaty pate with his sleeve. Adjusts his glasses. "It's … well, it's … hey, what are you doing right now? Why don't we have lunch?"

I want to protest, I almost do, but Larry's a good customer. Besides, Mr. B always says one should try, whenever possible, to treat other people with kindness. The golden rule and all that. I've done a great disservice to kindness over the years, so I might as well try to restore the balance to some degree. I don't believe Larry has many people in his life to eat lunch with.

"Sure, okay, lunch sounds good."

"Great." He smiles. It immediately turns into too wide of a grin. Larry is a grinner, and he shouldn't be. It kind of highlights the overall molest-ish vibe.

We go to Ruthie's. A local diner that does all the basics well, knows it, and sticks with it. Nothing fancy at Ruthie's, much to the chagrin of the local hipsters. Only two kinds of milk, a concession for the lactose intolerant, only two kinds of coffee: caf and decaf. Good, solid, easy choices. Ruthie's has been around forever, so long that it was originally named for the owner's daughter, then a child, and now a late-middle-aged woman with a bouffant hairdo and spirit to match, who operates the establishment. Mr. B orders from Ruthie's now and again. I've been in a few times on my own too. It's a quaint slice of Americana gone slightly to seed. The Formica countertops have seen kinder days, as have the checkered linoleum floors. But it's cozy. And affordable, a huge plus.

Larry orders a chicken fingers and fries platter with a mozzarella sticks starter. A soda to wash it all down with. I always did imagine the man's diet to be entirely fried. Funny how people tend to confirm your assumptions.

I order a club sandwich and a lemonade.

Larry makes something resembling small talk, waiting for the food to arrive, his grease-shiny fingers punctuating his statements about things like the weather. The meat of the conversation he seems to save for the main entrée.

"I belong to this club, you know … like a book club?"

Oh wow, I stand corrected, Larry does have friends.

"It's online."

Then again …

"So, we've all been reading *The Angelmaker* and doing some sleuthing and investigating of our own …"

Oh, boy.

"I mean, how can you not? The guy, for all we know, is still out there."

I nod. My sandwich is taking care of my end of the conversation.

I wish Larry was as diligent about using his napkin as he

is about his mastication. Alas, the napkin lies forgotten on the table. Larry is a loud eater; his lips are shiny with his lunch.

"So, if you adjust for age, profession, plausibility, and a bunch of other factors …" Larry pauses either for dramatic effect or because he finally realized his mouth is much too full to talk with. "How well do you know Mr. B?"

"What?" I nearly spurt my lemonade all over the guy. I did not expect that.

"Mr. B. A confirmed bachelor, a trusted community member, a man of superficial—" I bristle at that. "—charm. A man who was around at the time of the disappearances."

"Larry, that's …" I don't want to say crazy, because I've been on the receiving end of that particular blade one too many times, but if the shoe fits.

"You're gonna say crazy." He nods, pointing an accusing chicken finger my way. "I don't blame ya. You guys are close. But they had a suspect description at the time, and it matched Mr. B pretty closely."

"What? Like white man, medium height, medium build, thirties or forties? That's about half the male population here."

"He drove a blue car".

Mr. B has always driven blue cars, he loves the color blue.

"That proves nothing. You know how many blue cars are out there?"

"What about that story he wrote for the charity anthology? That was pretty creepy."

"What story?"

"It's online, you can look it up. Give ya nightmares."

"What, like a horror story?"

"Something like that."

"Well, plenty of people write those. Perfectly normal law-abiding people."

I'm actually kind of taken aback by this. How had I not known Mr. B had a story published? I didn't even know he wrote. I make a mental note to check it out.

"Well, I'm not saying nothing definitive," Larry

continues, "I'm just saying it's something to consider. Why not?"

"Why not? Because … because Mr. B is a good man." I can hear my voice going up an octave and struggle to bring it down. "Because he's done a lot for this community and for me and you don't get to … you don't get to sit around with your weirdo friends in your creepy club and speculate on this. It's wrong. It's just wrong."

No wonder Mr. B has never liked Larry. I'm through with pitying the guy. I finish my sandwich and pick up my glass to drain the last of lemonade. We're done here.

"Look, Jared, I'm sorry. I didn't mean to rile ya." He backpedals. "You tell me you never seen the guy acts weird around young women? Never seen or heard nothing weird about him?"

"Like what? Like if he walks around with an ax or has a hidden dungeon in the basement?"

For a quick second, Larry's eyes actually light up before

he realizes I'm making fun of him.

"All those effigies he made, all those angels. He might have something like that lying around, like a souvenir?"

I shake my head in muted disgust and signal for the check.

"Look, I'll get this, this is on me." Larry drags a beat-up leather billfold out of his pocket and pulls out a few bills. "I didn't mean to offend ya, Jared. You're always nice to me. I appreciate that. I don't want you to find yourself in a situation. I just … look, there's more to this suspicion that I have, that my friends have. Can you just …" He hands me a book. It's a mass-market paperback edition of *The Angelmaker*. I didn't even know there was one. He must have been just walking around with it. "Just read it, please. I highlighted some things. It won't take you any time, I bet you're a quick reader. Just read through this and tell me what you think."

He looks at me pleadingly. There's something pathetic about it. I want to look away. I want to leave.

"Please."

I sigh and take the book. If it's highlighted, I probably can't just put it back on the shelves and resell it, and I'd never toss a book, but maybe I'll stick it into one of those tiny libraries that have been cropping up —cute appropriations of abandoned newspaper boxes.

"Thanks, Jared. Really, thanks. This was … it's great. Thank you."

Poor guy, he's genuinely grateful for someone to share a meal with and to entertain his crazy theories.

"Sure, Larry. Thanks for lunch."

"Anytime, man. Maybe we can do it again sometime?"

In your wildest …

I smile noncommittally and vamoose. Where'd the sun go? It was blasting when we went into Ruthie's. Now it looks grey, like it might rain. I put the book in my bag and walk back to the bookstore. This afternoon off has certainly taken a strange turn.

There are none of those quaint tiny libraries on my way

back, though I look and look. Not a one. I do stop by the local deli, though. Back in the day, I'm not proud to say I stole from here. The bakery would drop off the fresh goods every morning on the deli's stoop before the place even opened, and I'd go by and liberate one or two. Some days it would be all I ate. Now I come in and shop here, paying more for things than I would in a local supermarket, offering my restitutions in a way.

Mr. B says it's all we can do. There's no balancing out the scales perfectly or precisely. Life moves on. The best you can do is try to do good going forth. Create your own justice, of sorts.

Works for me. I buy a small baguette and something for Mr. B. By the time I make it back to the store, I manage to put the awkward lunch with Larry out of my mind almost completely.

"Had a good time?"

"Had an okay time. How was the store?"

"Oh, you know, we got slammed, sold dozens of books. There are some shelves that are half-bare in the back, and I'm out of bookmarks."

It always takes me a moment—his delivery is so straight-faced.

"Hardy-har-har."

"A man can dream."

"Is that what you dream about?"

"No, young Annakin, I dream exclusively of Strawberry Yoo-hoos."

"Well then, you'll be pleased to know that I stopped by the deli and got you one."

"You're most considerate."

"And you … you made a *Star Wars* reference."

"Well, of course, I know *Star Wars*. I remember when it first came out. It was all anyone could talk about."

That was so long ago. I try to picture Mr. B as a young

man, but nothing comes. In my mind, his image is indelibly as it is now.

"Did you go see it?"

"You bet. Twice."

"Twice?" I smile.

"Wanted to make sure I got all the literary allusions."

Ah. "And did you?"

"Well, sure. The original got all your classic hero's journey three act structure straight out of Campbell. But really ..."

"Really?"

"It was just great fun."

Now that we can agree on.

"Got some cookies while you were out."

"Girl scouts again?"

"You bet."

Mr. B is determined to singlehandedly help those Girl Scouts meet their sales goals. And the Girl Scouts are well-aware of it. As a result, we always have entirely too many cookies. I cycle through favorites.

"They got a new flavor this year. You want to try it?"

I'm still full from my weird, weird lunch with Larry, but hey, I'm never going to say no to a cookie. I've so few vices left.

"Sure," I say. "Let me just throw my bag in my room."

I resolve not to mention the Larry thing to Mr. B. At first, I thought it would amuse him, but now I'm worried it might upset him. I can never tell these things, and it's always best to play it safe. After all, it really isn't worth mentioning.

I drop my bag on the floor of my room, put away my baguette and the lunch I packed but didn't get to eat, and hurry back, cookies on my mind.

That night I google Mr. B's story. It comes up quickly enough, something done for a charity anthology, creepy tales of our region, all proceeds went to a local wildlife refuge. I read it on one sitting.

Seaside

Every summer we, all of us, went to the seaside. Reluctantly giving in to the siren call of the waves, we followed the happy many to the sands and the sun, with all the correct accoutrements—sunscreens, books, sandwiches—and none of the concomitant joy seemingly experienced by those around us.

It's as if it was a ritual we had to uphold, a play at

normalcy, something set in motion once and committedly, if passionlessly, repeated since. A normal family takes summer vacations, and so there we were, though none of us had ever learned to swim, and all of us had the sort of paleness that has never met happily with the sun. There we were—father, perpetually misplacing his sunglasses, squinting at his latest historical tome, mother, adrift in thought and covertly snuck-in flask, and us three, unenthusiastically attempting to emulate the giddiness of the other children around us.

It was as if they were privy to some secret no one had thought to share with us. An impossible, unfathomable secret. Whatever wind had flown their kites and sailed their toy boats and battered the walls of their sandcastles eluded us completely. It seemed as though our family had its own climate and brought it along everywhere we went. I remember being aware of that strange disconnect even then, at an age where no such thoughts should cloud a young mind.   Yet we went on, a black and white silent movie amid the technicolor marathon around us.

Each year, the same seaside. Always returning, with mindless inexorability. Not as a response to the repeated, pleasingly rhythmic beating of the waves upon the shore, but as if driven by some darker, more primal thought and powered by some innate obduracy, a strange migration for migration's sake.

We fooled no one, not even ourselves. We never should have gone to the seaside. We didn't belong there, among the happy people. And so, it came as no surprise— not really— when one of us didn't come back.

My brother had been fascinated with photography ever since receiving his first camera as a birthday gift a few years before. My sister, his twin, received the same gift, as our parents were prone to a sort of meticulous unbiased evenness, but she never took to it. Shunned it, in fact. And yet, inadvertently she became my brother's greatest muse. The *shyest and most reluctant of all models, she would find herself giving in to his requests over and over again. She'd strike a pose, her eyes and her smile barely hiding her discomfort. Some of the images would be unposed—he'd simply sneak up on her as if hoping to glimpse something candid, something secret.*

I always believed that the reason behind my brother's obsession was a sort of vanity, for my sister was the closest reflection of him he could find anywhere outside of a mirror. They were uncannily alike, the two of them, lanky and tall, almost etiolated, pale, and fine-featured, with longish blonde hair and cloudy-sky grey eyes. They looked nothing like me, or I looked nothing like them, and this was perhaps why as a subject I had never interested my brother.

Or perhaps it was our age difference. Only a few short years, but often those prove to be insurmountable in childhood.

At any rate, it was always the two of them and then me,

as an afterthought. The two of them, the twins as similar in appearance as they were dissimilar in personalities. My brash, bold, and assertive brother and my mild, dreamy, quiet sister. I watched them with something approaching awe, but in passing years I've learned to recognize it as mere fawning adoration of the youngest sibling.

We weren't spoiled for choices when it came to company. Our house was much too isolated, and our schooling was done by our parents in an echoingly large, dusty library my father was so proud of. I didn't remember an age when I couldn't read. Books, it seems, were always an indelible part of my life. It was much the same for my sister, though she preferred hefty classics of bygone eras to my adventure stories.

My brother, out of all of us, was the one least likely to be satisfied with living his life vicariously through printed pages. No armchair adventurer, he longed for real-life quests and conquests. He went through phases of imagining himself as a polar explorer or an archeologist. Always in some faraway exotic destination. Photography was merely the latest incarnation of his interests, and while thus far my sister was his main subject, we all knew that when he got behind that viewfinder, he imaged distant islands and half-forgotten ruins of ancient civilizations. He was a restless spirit in a perfectly restful household, and it must have grated heavily upon his soul, though as a child I never gave it much thought.

I'd ask him to teach me, but he wouldn't. He wouldn't even utilize my help in his improvised darkroom in the basement. I'd sigh and pout, but soon go back to my books and my studies and forget all about it. Such are the pleasures of childhood when thoughts can flit and pass instead of lingering unwelcomingly or settling down to wear heavily upon their thinker.

At some point in our studies, my sister became interested in the Indigenous cultures and their beliefs. It is there, among the folklore and myths, that she found the most likely explanation for her camera shyness. "It steals your soul," she'd tell our brother. "Every moment you still the time with your camera, you steal some of my essence," she'd say.

He didn't take her seriously, of course, dismissing her concerns as superstition and silliness. My brother's confidence had always made him callous. He wasn't mean, I don't think, just careless. Which now that I'm older, I know can be just the same.

When my sister became slimmer, when her eyes acquired dark shadows beneath them, I couldn't say. But then, speaking from the retrospective perch of my later years, teenage girls are prone to drama, aren't they? I noticed the changes in her, but didn't think much of it, not then.

In those days my brother was determined to develop a portfolio of his work. His compositions got more and more ambitious. He even included me in some of them. It was as if he was trying to tell stories with his photos, stories of great adventures the likes of which I devoured in our library and *late at night, after lights out, in my own bed. We were great explorers or guileless locals, we were pharaohs and kings and pyramid builders, soldiers, and victims.*

A photo shoot of my sister as Cleopatra was my brother's magnum opus. He must have spent all of his allowance on props, things he couldn't build or repurpose from the house. It came out beautifully, it stands to mention. Hauntingly beautiful, in retrospect. My sister had never looked more beautiful and less like herself. Her fair hair hidden away by a stylized black wig, her fair eyes rimmed in heavy makeup. She looked royal, she looked regal. Even our parents, in their hands-off approach to our hobbies, were impressed when those photos were developed.

Afterward, my sister took to her room for a week, claiming weakness. I brought her meals and books and thought she did look weak, more ephemeral somehow.

When she recovered, she begged my brother to no longer photograph her, and he acquiesced, for a while, but in the end, he went right back to it, dismissing her concerns, overriding her protests the way he tended to.

She never told our parents about this, or if she did, they didn't do a thing about it. I was never quite sure. Our parents lived a very separate life from ours. It was as if we existed in adjacent, parallel but not interconnected universes. They made sure we were clothed, fed, and educated. They disciplined us, but never harshly. They never raised their voices. It was almost as if they were puzzled by us, by our existence, like we were a fundamentally different species, something to tolerate, take care of, be bemused by, but never really, profoundly engage with. There was always that distance that made you question the existence of love. I was sure they loved each other, they seemed perfectly matched. I just was never sure they loved us. Cared for us, sure, but those are two very different things.

That day at the beach my brother had the idea to create a

photo shoot of some famous ruins. We were meant to be the fallen statues. He included me too, but the focus, as always, was mostly on my sister. She was reluctant as always and, as always, my brother's will persevered and won out. He displayed her on the beach, at the line where the sea hungrily lapped at the sand before reluctantly retreating. A calming, repetitive motion, made somewhat sinister by the grey threatening skies of the day. Made more sinister still by the great quantity of seaweeds tangled in the water, so that it seemed as if in some bizarre role reversal the sea was fishing for people. Trying to drag them back with its weed-woven nets.

My sister was to lie there, half-buried by sand, eyes downcast, her alabaster skin a perfect stand-in for a long-abandoned statue. I merely watched. Watched as my brother took shot after shot, varying his angles. Watched as the wind gained strength around us. Watched as the skies grew darker. And yet, somehow, I managed to miss noticing the waves increasing in size and threat. They all must have missed it, because out of nowhere came a great wave that covered my sister entirely. When it retreated, my sister was gone.

There was no scream, no sound at all outside of the rushing sea. We searched, of course, we searched. People came and searched with us. And in the end, they departed, and we were left all alone in our bewildered grief. "The sea takes what it wants," they said. They were right, the sea never gave us my sister back. She never washed ashore like a discarded shell. She was just ... gone. It was speculated that she must have gotten caught in the weeds and dragged under, but I never believed it. Not then and not now.

Afterward, I remember seeing my brother's photos of that day, the last images he ever took of her, and I swear she looked paler than ever, almost translucent. I knew then without being able to put words to it that he really did somehow steal her soul with all his photographs, just like he stole some of her spirit every time he disregarded her request for privacy.

She wasn't his to take, no matter how strong their twin connection was, no matter how much they might have seemed to an outsider like obverse sides of the same coin, like mirrored images of each other. I grieved for my sister with the fierceness of a first-time loss. It shaped me, molded me, stole away my childhood. My parents weren't much comfort, nor did I expect them to be, and so I was all alone in my sadness.

We didn't go back to the seaside that summer. But the following year, my parents must have deemed that the intervening year had been an appropriate time allotment for grief, and back we went. It wasn't the same, I never thought it would be. But my brother was trying to make the best of it. The last year had matured him. He was beginning to look more like the man he was destined to become than the boy he was leaving behind. He was shaving already. Talking of universities. Imagining and planning for the life my sister never got to have.

He was trying to be kind to me then, I could tell. He let me play with his beloved camera, he tried helping me build a sandcastle. He even let me bury him in the sand with only his head sticking out until he looked like a living version of a sarcophagus. I piled the sand higher and higher, and he laughed, saying he couldn't move now if he tried.

I looked at our parents. They were lost to their reading. I continued to pile more sand. And then I sat back and waited for the waves to come. The sea obliged.

I didn't mind being the only child for the rest of my years under my parents' roof. Sometimes I think they were secretly relieved. One was so much more manageable than three. They never changed the way they behaved toward me: there was no warmth before, and none later. They did their best and sent me off to a top-tier university the first chance they got. Living away for the first time proved terrifying and exhilarating at the same time. Once I learned the ways of the world, I learned to thrive in it. It was vast and splendid, and I think my sister, had she lived, would have liked it very much.

Citing reasons of privacy, I managed to avoid having my picture taken whenever possible. And I never went to the seaside again.

I've no idea what to make of it. It's pretty good, I think, nicely atmospheric. But it's just a story, isn't it? Who knows what Larry's disturbed imagination had twisted it into? Who knows what his friends make of it when they dissect it for meaning?

There's a certain haunting quality to the story that I like and wouldn't mind having a chat about, but I figure if Mr. B wanted to talk about it, he would have brought it up a long time ago. I certainly don't know how to bring it up to him.

Can't just say, "Oh, by the way, I googled you and found a short story you wrote years ago. Care to discuss your motivations and narrative choices?"

No, no way, not doing that. I resolve then and there never to mention it to Mr. B. After all, we have enough stories around us already.

If I had a dad, I'd want him to be just like Mr. B. He doesn't have any kids as far as I know, and I've no idea if he'd ever want a son like me. But to me, he's always been something of a parent figure, maybe a parent/friend is a more accurate way to explain it. At the very least, he's been avuncular. I'm an apprentice and protégé and an assistant rolled into one, but it's more than that too. I've always been a fan of the concept of a chosen family as opposed to the inherited one, and if given a choice, I'd always choose Mr. B. He's got a way about him, he cares without saying it, guides without patronizing. I know with dead certainty that I'm a better person because of him. And yet I'd never say any of that to him because it's just not how we talk. Or what we talk about. Instead, we talk about books and sometimes …

"Look at that goofy furball. What kind of breed is that?"

We're people-watching together, a reward of leisure time after processing a sizeable donation. The store is empty and has been for most of the day. We're in the ebb of the ebb and flow of bookselling. All we have to do is turn our chairs to the glass storefront wall and observe. It's lunch hour, and the street is relatively busy. This is how I like life—observed from a safe remove. I spent too much time on the outside looking in, the reverse situation is infinitely more preferable.

"It's a Pomeranian," says Mr. B. "They didn't always use to look like that. You can thank Queen Victoria for this version."

"How come?"

"Back in her day they were a medium-size breed, but she got a smaller one and decided that should be the standard and had them bred accordingly."

"Oh, to be the queen," I try to joke.

"Indeed. The power to mess with all sorts of things."

We sit quietly for a while. Watch people navigate the puddles from the overnight rain.

"Tell me a story," I say, because it's what we do.

"Mm, okay, well, once upon a time, a Seattle bookseller by the name of Richard Weatherford developed the first online database for used and rare books. This was back in 1993. The business of bookselling was still booming, and he thought to amplify that boom. So did everyone else. Ironically enough, his database, Interloc, was financed by booksellers themselves. And then the following year, a Wall Street trader named Bezos borrowed a quarter or so of a million dollars from his parents and started an online bookstore out of a rented house in Washington. That's Washington state, not DC. A couple of months later, he's selling books to all fifty states, making thousands a month. And now we're sitting here, twiddling our thumbs because the internet is trying to steal away all our customers."

"Ah, a sad story."

"A true story. All true stories have some sadness to them."

I nod. I people-watch some more. But Mr. B has turned his attention on me.

"You sleeping okay, kid?"

"Yeah, yes, why do you ask?"

"You got those black undereye circles again."

I'm not going to mention that for the past week I've had trouble sleeping. Fact is, I'm doing my best to put it out of my mind with every waking moment. I bought construction-grade earplugs. I diligently ignore any and all noises of the night, especially those that sound like voices. There will be no angelic visitations for me. No more. I am the master of my fate and all that.

I'm tired, I'm tired every day. My sleep is restless and uneven. It takes me longer to do simple tasks, my reading has slowed to a crawl—my mind drifts and tries to doze, and I end up spending much too long on each page. But at the end of every day, I feel like a warrior who fought a battle against madness and won.

"I've been sleeping kinda weirdly," I prevaricate noncommittally.

"Try melatonin. It's all-natural."

I promise I'll look into it. Whatever takes my mind off the fact that this morning Larry's paperback copy of *The Angelmaker* has materialized on my ersatz nightstand. I'm 100% sure I never took it out of my bag. I don't want to think about what that might mean.

Larry hasn't been back since our lunch the other week. For that I'm glad. The customers come and go, some regulars, some newcomers. A woman who's been pregnant seemingly for as long as I can remember comes in with a newborn tucked away into a wraparound fabric carrier. Mr. B and I coo all the appropriate coos, tell her we hope the baby will be a reader like his mom. Secretly, I hope the baby will have better taste than his mom, who has been steadily working her way through Danielle Steel's back catalog.

"Well, there's her life, all sorted," says Mr. B after she leaves.

"How do you mean?"

"She's a mother now, that's her life, 24/7. Every gene in her body is telling her that's the most important job she'll ever have. She'll kill for that baby now."

That reminds me of something, something I saw and wanted to discuss with him.

"I watched a documentary the other day about former Nazis ... " I start.

"Interesting." Mr. B nods, ever the history buff.

"A bunch of them immigrated to other countries, got new names, and went on to have perfectly normal lives. Like suburbs, white picket fences, 2.4 kids, the works. It just … it boggled my mind."

"Everyone gets a chance at a second act."

"What if people don't deserve it? What if what they've done in their first one is too horrid?"

"Well, deserve is a funny word. Difficult to ascribe value to, too malleable. Did they become law-abiding citizens since? Did they contribute to the society going forth? Think about personal value. And while we're on the subject of World War II, think about all the Nazi scientists that the US took in, all the people that helped further scientific progress in their respective fields. Should they have been arrested and shot instead?"

Somehow, he always manages to reframe the question. The man would have killed on a debate team.

"So, they just do what they want and get away with it,

scot-free?"

"I don't believe for a second it's as simple as that, son. A guilty conscience is the heaviest of weights to lug around."

How would he know? The man probably never got so much as a speeding ticket. He told me he was fortunate enough to avoid going to war, that college saved him. His conscience is probably crystal clear. Mine, I'm not so sure. To be honest, I can't even remember some of what I've done, that's how messed up I was back then. There are times I look back at my life and all I see is missing time, lost memories. I was the blackout drunk who never cared to find out what he did the night before. My life back then was merely an accumulation of occurrences, with no structure, meaning, or sequence to them. How far I've come. How much I have to fear backsliding.

"You ever notice how people refer to them as former Nazis?" Mr. B brings me back out of my gloomy reverie. "No one ever says a former killer. The linguistics themselves seem to imply the deed was in the past and that it was, in fact, a deed, not a character trait."

"Mm, good point."

"I'm full of those." He smiles. "Chinese for lunch?"

Later, my stomach comfortably weighted down by noodles and sodium, I take a walk around the neighborhood, hoping that the fresh air will wake me up. It does the trick, somewhat.

Night comes earlier these days, but I love the way the bookstore looks in the evening, like a beacon at sea, a warm beckoning light in the darkness, guiding me home. I always wanted that feeling, that sense of belonging. I think I started to believe I deserved it, but now in these moments when I'm all alone with my thoughts, I feel fear reaching in and squeezing my heart with its icy fingers. I think about angels and shifting books and I'm so, so afraid that it's the beginning of some tragic unraveling of all the carefully woven fabric of my life. I shiver and hurry back, still tired but no longer sleepy.

Sometimes one of the earplugs finds its way out of my ears no matter how diligently I jab them in. And that's probably why the voice that night is impossible to ignore.

"Jared."

"Pssst, Jared."

I moan, roll over and try to roll my pillow around my ears.

"Jared." I feel a tug on my pillow. That's new. It works as effectively as a bucket of ice water. Now I'm awake. I sit up and dig the other earplug out. Wait for my eyes to adjust to the darkness.

"You've been ignoring us." The voice sounds less accusatory than sad.

"I just wanted some peace."

"So do we, Jared, so do we."

"I can't … I can't help you."

"You can. You will."

"How?"

"Read the book."

"What?"

"Read. The. Book."

I play for time. "What book?"

There's an audible whoosh, and the next thing I know I'm hit in the face with a paperback. A distinctly unpleasant sensation no matter how much you love books.

I pick it up, but I don't have to see the cover. It is, of course, *The Angelmaker*.

"You threw the book at me? Literally?" *That's kind of funny, isn't it?*

The angels are not in the mood.

"Read the book, Jared," they say once more in a voice that sounds like many, and then there's just silence. I guess they're gone for the night.

I don't turn on the light. I don't even move. I sit in my bed contemplating what this means. It hasn't eluded me that the angels now have a new trick up their sleeve. They can move objects. What that bodes for me and my sanity, I don't know.

But I know one thing with absolute certainty. They won't stop. And so, there's really only one thing I can do. I sigh, put on the light, and begin to read the book.

In the 1980s, for the only time in its history, our town made the national news. It was also the only time in its history that our town was ever considered unsafe. It started slowly and quietly with a crime that almost went unnoticed because it almost went unregistered as a crime.

Toni Valence was an eighteen-year-old high-school dropout with dyed pink hair, technicolor tattoos, and an attitude to match. She worked at a local tattoo parlor and lived with her mom in a beat-up trailer on the edge of town. When she disappeared one day, it took her mom days to sober up enough to realize this was an unusual behavior even for her hurricane of a daughter—who raised storms in teacups but always stayed put—and report it to the police. The police were disinclined to help. Toni was legally an adult. If she wanted to flee her dead-end life, it was certainly her choice. Her mother protested, her employer protested —Toni of all things was mid-tattoo at the time of her disappearance, an elaborate backpiece a week away from completion—but the protestations fell on deaf ears. The town didn't care. The town moved on.

Jenny Grover was an eighteen-year-old high school senior, a nice quiet girl who loved movies and worked part-time at the local movie theater. She had the look of someone who'd go the distance to avoid notice, a mousy girl who preferred her adventures to be of a cinematic variety. She didn't even really enjoy traveling, her parents would say later. Why would she ever just take off?

Unlike Mrs. Valence, the Grover family were a respected local presence, owners and operators of a small accounting business, and police had no choice but to take their complaints seriously. But once again, there was no evidence of any wrongdoing and Jenny was, shy or not, of age, so the case went nowhere.

Lila Moore was a vivacious seventeen-year-old with a bright future. That's how people who knew her described her, anyway. She excelled in English and history and planned to attend the state university and become a high school teacher. She got along with her parents, volunteered at a local pet shelter, had friends and a boyfriend, a local football star. She was smiling in all her pictures, always. A blonde and sunny and happy girl. Not the sort of girl who'd ever just disappear. Not the sort of girl you wouldn't notice disappearing. Plus, at only seventeen, she was officially a minor.

Now the police investigation could proceed in full force. Now the connections began being made. Now the townspeople started to get scared.

The thing is, though, there was nothing to be done. There

were no official crime scenes to investigate. If the girls were taken from their homes, there was no evidence to support it. No evidence *at all*. The girls were just vanishing into thin air, it seemed. Taken, stolen from their lives. People around them were checked out and found to be whistle-clean. No one knew anything. Meanwhile, more girls went missing.

Precautions were suggested. Then enforced. Later came a curfew. But young people had the invincibility of youth on their side and threw caution to the wind. Sometimes at their peril. When the number of suspected victims hit half a dozen, the FBI came in. Their serious, somber, dark-suited presence punctuated the town's streets.

By then the entire ambiance was changing. Suddenly, there was a sense of living in dangerous times. People hunkered down. Gun sales went up.

And then … it just stopped. As suddenly as it began. The girls simply stopped disappearing. The town held a collective breath for a while and then slowly, gratefully released it. It was over. It was all over.

Not for the families of the missing girls, of course. For them, the nightmare went on and never ended. The debilitating uncertainly of never knowing. Mrs. Valence had drunk herself to death a few years later. The Grovers divorced. The Moores adopted a young girl from China. People grieved differently.

The fact was, the world they thought they knew turned around and surprised them, showed them a face so unforgettably ugly as to scar a psyche for life. And nothing was quite the same after, even though everyone did their best to pretend to go back to normal.

And worst of all was the fact that the perpetrator was never caught. The only thing even making the disappearances into official crimes, the only thing unifying them as a potential work of the same person were the angel effigies later found in the girls' rooms. Mrs. Valence thought it was a creepy doll from her daughter's creepy doll collection and never even reported it at first. The Moores and the Grovers knew their daughters better. And from then on it was easy to look for and always there to find. A crude figure no larger than a Barbie doll, made with some skill, but not a work of proper craftsmanship, for there was something undeniably crude about it, the angel effigy was a construct of roughly carved wood and wire, the wings were made of real feathers—pigeon, nothing exotic. Nothing about the production was unique enough to be easily placed, all the components could be easily found in local woods or maybe even a park. The wire was a sort available in any hardware store. For all the simplicity of the effigy, there was something inherently creepy about it, but that might have just been the confirmation bias at work. Had it been found at a local craft fair you'd likely not give it a second thought.

No evidence, no bodies … and so, the case remained

unsolved. The FBI spun its wheels with growing frustration for a while longer, then left. Things settled down into the monotonous comforting quietude for years to come.

Until the letter.

It arrived at the local newspaper, a single typed and printed sheet, well-edited and in legible font. Its author claimed responsibility for the disappearances. It wasn't an apology so much as a confession, the goal of which was to give the families much-needed closure.

The girls were dead, the letter said, in a matter-of-fact tone. Their deaths were quick. "They are with the angels now. There will be no more." Signed, The Angelmaker.

A collective band-aid the entire town had worn for years was ripped away, revealing a still oozing wound. It was all anyone could or would talk about. The FBI came back. But, of course, the letter much as the effigies before it, was as evidence-free as a gust of wind. Was it a hoax, some people wanted to know? How much easier it would have been if it was. Alas, the letter provided some details only the person responsible would know. It was determined to be genuine, almost certainly written by the perpetrator. Beyond that, the investigation went nowhere.

Ultimately, nothing changed. Although the families did get their closure, they weren't given bodies to bury, places to mourn. It was a resolution, of sorts. It was the best they were going to get. Another collective sigh, another collective band-aid, and the town, once again, made a valiant effort to move on. It was over, it was really over this time, they told themselves.

And that's the gist of *The Angelmaker*. Not a large book—there simply isn't enough material available to justify the word count and only so much speculation to pad the pages. It's comprehensive and slightly ghoulish in its pruriency, but such things are to be expected from the true crime genre.

People want a window into the most aberrant of psyches, the most devastating of tragedies, a glimpse into the abyss from the safety of their armchairs. But they prefer those things to come with neat resolutions, something they can weigh, measure, and dismiss as "not in their world" so that they can go back to their illusion of safety. The Angelmaker case refused to offer a neat solution and thus permanently embedded itself into the morbid imaginations of genre aficionados and amateur crime solvers. It was one of the latter variety that wrote the book.

To his credit, it wasn't terrible. It was surprisingly readable, in fact, though I admittedly didn't have many similar books to compare it to. Ultimately, though, I didn't learn much more than Larry had told me, for there simply wasn't much more to learn.

I read until dawn—sleep no longer being an option—and finished the book just in time for breakfast. I'm tired, so tired that it's difficult to hold on to any individual thought for long.

There is something about the book that's nagging me, some small detail, but try as I might, I can't bring it into focus.

Maybe after coffee, I think, trying to wash exhaustion out of my face. Maybe then.

Today's Pop-Tart flavor is cherry. Mr. B is in a good mood. I'm too sleepy to have a mood.

"Still not sleeping?"

"Not much," I admit, sipping my coffee.

"Did you try melatonin?"

"I'll get some today."

"Walking. They say walking helps too. Fresh air. I know your room doesn't get any. I wonder if we need to have a window installed there. Maybe I can get a quote? I know a guy."

I do my best to assure him that no window is needed. I don't want to put him out. He's already done so much for me and is doing so much for me still.

As it turns out, the reason for Mr. B's good mood is a

write-up the store got in a travel magazine's recent issue. "Small Towns, Hidden Treasures" or something like that. I get online to check it out and sure enough, there we are. A nice photo and a quick glowing review.

"I think I'll cut it out and frame it," he says.

There's something endearingly old-fashioned about it. I tell him I think that's a good idea. There are already a few framed photos on the walls—the local newspaper's article from when the store opened and from its 10th anniversary, a couple of shots with local authors who did signing events here. We haven't done one of those in a while. Not many authors are from here, I suppose.

The day crawls as my brain desperately tries to snap into something like alertness. The Angelmaker book is doing laps around my cerebral cortex, bouncing up and down, refusing to sit still. That nagging detail, that thing I can't place, is driving me crazy. It was something among all the baseless speculation, which, to be fair to Larry, did include an elaborate criminal profile composed by a prominent local psychologist broad enough to technically include Mr. B as well as a good majority of the male population of our town in it. It's the same thing they say about all serial killers, isn't it? White, educated, financially stable, superficially charismatic, intelligent, etc., etc.

At a squint, even Larry could be slated into that box. But no, he'd never pass the charisma test, superficial or not. He hasn't been around though. I hope it isn't because of our lunch—I don't miss the guy, but I can't be turning away business from the store, not these days.

I don't want to think about all that anymore. I turn to Mr. B and say, "Tell me a story." The man is all too glad to oblige.

He tells me a story of an Englishman named Richard Booth – an eccentric who had so loved books that he created a kingdom of them. The people around him didn't take too kindly to it and so, after a run-in with the Wales Tourist Board, Booth declared the town Hay-on-Wye an independent kingdom and appointed himself its King.

"Unbelievable." I shake my head. "And this was when?"

"1977, if memory serves. You think that's too much, well, he made his horse his Prime Minister."

Nice one, I think.

"For years," Mr. B goes on, "Booth would confer titles on people for a modest fee. His cabinet meetings took place monthly at a local pub, and topics were chosen by spinning a game show-type wheel that featured entries like "have a drink," "defer to the next session,", or "chop off her head." Booth also operated a local intelligence agency, CIHay. Whoever brought him the juiciest gossip was rewarded with a royal title and a pint of Guinness."

Ah, I like this Booth guy, just the right kind of kooky.

"What happened to him?

"Old age."

"Bet he died happy."

"One can certainly hope so. At the very least, he lived happily enough."

"Hay-on-Wye. Is it still there? Still in business?"

"You bet. The best lil' book town in the world, so they say."

"You've never been?"

"No. Not yet, anyway."

"Would you like to?"

"Oh, I'm not much of a traveler. Something about this town got its hooks into me, and I can't seem to ever leave, even for a short while. I'm afraid it's armchair travel for me, exclusively."

I nod, I get it, it's the same for me.

"So, you read about this Hay place?"

"Yeah, it's got some interesting history to it, the way

small British towns tend to. The only British solicitor to ever be hanged for murder was from there."

"You don't say."

"I do say." He smiles. It's a thing we do. "Armstrong was his name. The fool poisoned his wife with arsenic. The most Victorian of all crimes, though this was a couple of decades after The Queen's passing. People saw him buy it and all."

"Couldn't have been a very good solicitor, then," I say.

"Certainly made a stupid criminal."

"And so, he hanged."

"By the neck until he was dead."

"Ah."

Just like that, once again, Mr. B has succeeded in dragging my mind out of its dark shadows and into the daylight. The rest of the day passes by in a much nicer ambiance. I finally feel fully awake after lunch—it's only cheap Mexican fare, but the spices do the trick.

Only toward the store's closing, while I'm sweeping the floors and resettling any books that got jostled by careless customers during the day, does it hit me like a slap on the face. That tiny nagging detail … it comes to me, vividly. That famous Angelmaker effigy, the one prominently featured on the cover, I know where I saw something eerily similar. And in that moment, all I want to do is unknow that fact.

It's not that easy, though—not when you're clean and sober—to just put something out of your mind. I've been trying and failing to do that for years, with my life, with Cherry, and now with all this angel business. Some days I just wish I could wake up every morning with a clean slate, like that Drew Barrymore character in an old rom-com with her weird amnesia. Or be able to put my past in the basement and never go there, like Mr. Ripley, whose murder-tinged adventures I'm reading about currently, based on Mr. B's recommendation.

But no, I get to drag it around with me, like a heavy weight threatening to pull me under. More baggage than a train station. I am so, so very tired of it.

I've only once been to Mr. B's apartment. He never visits

my room either. We respect each other's personal spaces and spend enough time together during the day, each day, to merit privacy in the evenings. And so, I had only visited his humble abode once, when his bathroom pipes burst and flooded a section of the store. He needed help shutting off the water, the lever got stuck, the plumber was still some time away. It was a hectic time, and I didn't exactly get a tour of the place, but I took some of it in.

It was much as expected: comfortable, in an understated way, clean, neat as a pin. Nothing new, nothing fancy, but cozy in its own way. A place I could see him being happy in. A place I could see myself being happy in. I remember feeling glad he had a home like that, nothing like a place some people his age might end up in; no old people smells, no clutter, no aggregations of decades of knickknacks and old photos. Just simple practical things—a couch, a television, a record player and some records, bookshelves with books on them.

That's why it stood out, the strange thing that at the time

I took for a dolly. It wasn't prominently displayed—I only noticed it because I bumped into a bookcase, knocked down some books, and saw the dolly sitting behind. A crude, strange-looking thing. At the time, I barely gave it a second thought. Now it's all I can think about. About how much it resembles the freaking angel effigy.

I pick up the book from my nightstand and stare at its cover. My practical logical brain matter tells me it's nothing at all at best and a pastiche at most. Something he may have seen in the news and tried to imitate to appease some morbid corner of his psyche. Or not even that—maybe a strange gift from someone, or a weird find among the book donations that he never brought himself to dispose of. It could be anything.

And then there's another part of my brain, the sleep-deprived, angel-haunted one that tells me it could only be one thing.

I'm torn, sad, mad, tired and I don't know how, but I manage to doze off, because the next thing I know it's the middle of the night—angel o'clock—and there they are, whispering to me.

"I read your freaking book. I hope you're happy."

"We haven't been happy in a long time, Jared."

Right.

"But we are pleased you're finally taking us seriously."

"It proves nothing."

"Then why are you so upset?"

"Because ..." I start loudly and then force myself to exhale and lower my voice, "because this is upsetting. All of this. You're messing with my mind, making me question what I know, planting suspicions against a good man. A *good* man. The best man I know."

"We thought he was a good man too, once. Look at us now."

I shake my head.

"LOOK AT US." It isn't a scream as such, but it reverberates in my head all the same. I look up. And sure enough, I can see … something. Rough outlines of young women, maybe. Or maybe a stress-induced hallucination. Who's to tell.

"Why … How? How come I can see you now?"

"Your mind is opening up, Jared. It's an uncomfortable but necessary step."

"I don't suppose I have any say in the matter."

"Jared, this will all be over soon. Our time draws near. Don't fight it. Don't fight us, help us."

I look at them, then at the book, that terrible, terrible paperback of doom. For the first time in my life, I want to do violence to a book, I want to burn it—a notion antithetical to all my values, and yet there it is. But then again, of course, it isn't the book's fault.

"You know what to do next," the angels tell me.

"I do?"

But they are gone. The Irish Goodbye all over again, their specialty. What they leave me with … it's too much.

I toss the book in the trash bin, it's the least damage, and possibly the most, that I can do to it. It brings me no peace.

It's Mr. B's volunteering day. He used to do more of it—giving back to the community is pretty high on his list of moral codes and values—but now with his age taking its toll and his mobility growing increasingly limited, he has finally slowed down. This is the one thing he still does, happily, teaching the adult literacy class at the local library.

He takes a cab there, and I'm left all alone to mind the store. Normally, it wouldn't even phase me, but today isn't a normal day. Today is a day I woke up to find a book I clearly remember throwing into the trash sitting right next to my head on my pillow. For the third morning in a row.

I get it, angels, I get it. Though I positively loathe what I have to do next, do it I must.

I know where Mr. B keeps a spare key. He showed me once, after I had been at the bookstore for a while. It was like a trust fall on his behalf and I appreciated it—it had been a long time since anyone had trusted me. It had been a long time since I'd been considered trustworthy by anyone, including myself.

It was a trust I swore to myself I'd never abuse. And look at me now, reaching below the register for the beat-up hardcover copy of *Oliver Twist* and retrieving a key taped to the inside of it. I hate myself.

I hate myself as I lock up the store with a "Back in 15" sign, I hate myself as I creep up the stairs to Mr. B's apartment, and I hate myself as I turn the key and let myself in. Just one quick look, I tell myself, one quick look, and I'll leave. One quick look that'll put paid to all my paranoid ideations and set me free.

It has occurred to me that perhaps this was all just an elaborate self-sabotage scheme that my faulty brain has cooked up. What if it can't function on that high of a contentment setting? What if it needs drama, despair, destitution? What if it's trying to rip up this comfortable rug I found myself on from under my feet, trip me up, send me back to the time before?

What if? What if? What if?

Stop.

I make a beeline straight for the bookcase, move some books aside, and there it is. A crude ugly dolly made of reclaimed wood and wire and feathers. Instantly and devastatingly recognizable from the book, it's impossible to deny it was done by the same hands.

As I stand there staring at it, I can feel something, some purely somatic goodness, just leaving me. I don't know how to describe it. You know the way a hot shower feels after being outside for hours on a blustery bitter winter day? Well, this feeling is the opposite of that. Like all comfort at once vacating the premises. What's left is nothing—ice in my veins, stones in my heart.

Somewhere in a distant corner of my psyche, a small

voice tells me that there might still be a rational explanation for all of this. Maybe Mr. B knew The Angelmaker; maybe it was his friend, or his secret son, or something. Maybe he held on to this grotesque memento out of some misguided obligation or misplaced affection for the person. Maybe …

I can't indulge in these thoughts, not now, there's no time. I put everything back just as I had found it and leave as quickly and quietly as I had come in. Back downstairs, I take the sign off, unlock the store, get back behind the counter like it's business as usual. Like my heart hasn't just been ripped out.

I check the wall clock. It's a novelty item, its face is decorated with vintage book spines. Its hands tell me Mr. B will be back soon. I have less than an hour to get back to normal, at least to act normal. How difficult will it be, knowing what I know now? How difficult has it been for Mr. B all these years, living with his secret? And he seems so … nice, happy, normal.

Away from the angels, away from that terrible book,

away from that horrid dolly. How can I possibly think that he might have done all those things to all those girls? Do I really believe that the man who had singlehandedly saved my life could have ended so many others?

I think I act okay when he gets back, casual-like, business-as-usual-like. I ask all the right questions, show the right amount of interest. Smile when he tells me about the progress he is making with Teddy, a man recently released from prison and determined to, at last, turn his life around for the sake of his newborn daughter. Say thank you when he produces a box of donuts from our favorite donut shop, eat the blueberry one without tasting it. Normal, normal, normal—as the day stretches out impossibly long, and I will the clock hands to move faster toward the closing time. Normal, normal, normal—until we lock up, and I say goodnight and go to my room.

The book is back on my pillow, though I'm sure I threw it under the bed before I left. I'm not hungry. I'm not tired. I lay down on the bed without so much as taking off my shoes. The donut is sitting heavily in my gut, tasting like a lie.

I wait for them; I wait for the angels.

I can see them much clearer now. I can make out each individual feature. They look just like the girls from the photos in the book. Because, of course, they do.

"You saw it."

"I saw it."

"You believe?"

"Either that, or I'm going crazy."

"You're not going crazy."

"That's just what all crazy people tell themselves."

Silence for a beat. An impasse, of sorts.

"You can always just ask him."

"Just ask him? Like, "Hey, Mr. B. Thanks for the coffee. By the way, did you happen to abduct some girls back in the eighties?"

"And kill," they hiss.

"And kill," I amend.

They nod.

"It's my life. You understand that, right? It's my entire life I'd be throwing away. A life *he* gave me. A home, a job, a friendship. All for what? To satisfy you?"

"For justice, Jared."

"And when he laughs me out of the store and out of his life, then what? Will be happy at last? Because you'll be all alone then, with no one to haunt, no one to whisper nightmares to in the middle of the night."

"You need to get him to admit what he did. You need to get him to tell people where he hid us. Then we can be free."

"Why'd it take you so long? You've just been here since the eighties, waiting for a sucker like me?"

"No one could hear us before, no one could see us before."

"So, I'm special then?"

"Yes, Jared, you are."

I was afraid of that. All I ever wanted to be was ordinary.

"And if I can't? If I won't?"

"Then we'll persist. We'll never leave you alone. We'll make you question every single thing in your life. You'll never know a moment of peace."

Suddenly, the angels sound all too much like demons. Suddenly, I fear them, genuinely fear them.

"How would I even …?"

"At least get the effigy from his apartment. It's evidence. Give it to someone. Tell someone."

I consider this for a moment. What a monumental stab in the back this would be. Could I ever do such a thing? Could I live with myself as I did?

"Like the cops?"

"Yes, Jared, like the cops."

I contemplate this scenario. "It'll never work. I have a rap sheet. I have a history of psychiatric disturbances. No one is going to listen to a word I say."

That gives them pause at last and me a minute to catch my breath. At long last, my reputation as a world-class fuck-up had come in handy.

"Bring it to us, then," they say after a while. "We'll figure it out."

"And then you'll leave me alone?" Do I dare hope …

"And then we'll see."

Well, I suppose it's my best and only chance of getting rid of them, I'll take it.

I have to wait until Mr. B has his volunteering thing next. A tense week of walking on hot coals of anticipation, but at least the angels in their infinite manipulative mercy leave me alone. I even manage some sleep, and Mr. B compliments my improved complexion.

"Your birthday's coming up, old sport. We should celebrate. Do something special. There's a new restaurant that's just opened, right down the street from the library. Fusion something, if you fancy that sort of thing."

His words, his kindness feel like daggers to my traitorous heart. I've done my best to act normal this entire time, but it's taking its toll. I overthink every sentence, every gesture. I'd never make it as a spy. I stress-sweat through a shirt by the afternoon these days.

At last, he leaves, and I reach for the key. Repeat my clandestine ascent to his apartment, my unwelcome visit. The dolly—"the effigy," I recall the angels whisper—is where it was last, waiting for me. I reach for it, but my hands refuse to touch it as if they have a mind of their own. I have to take off my button-down shirt and use it to take the wood-and-wire figure and wrap it up. It's probably smarter that way anyway, it occurs to me, because of the fingerprints. And then the thought echoes in my mind, like a mea culpa on repeat. The effigy feels heavier than it ought to, or maybe that's just my guilt.

I turn to leave and there he is, Mr. B. Standing in the door, watching me. I had no idea when he got there or how he did it so quietly. Guess he didn't use his cane.

"Something you wanna tell me, kid?" he asks casually.

If I could vanish into the thin air right now, I would. Just disappear, have the universe gobble me up, and spit me out somewhere in another dimension with no angels or effigies or horrible suspicions marring my friendships.

Alas, no such thing. I remain stock-still and deer-in-the-headlights startled, still clutching the stupid doll.

"I thought I heard a noise," I say lamely and after much too much time passes. "I came up to see if …"

"You came up to valiantly defend my property by … using my property?" He points to the bundle in my arms, seemingly amused.

"Something like that," I nod. *Stupid, stupid.* "No, I mean, this was on the floor, I picked it up and wrapped it up so it wouldn't get damaged." *Oh man, I am a terrible liar.*

"Well, thank you for your vigilant service, I suppose. I'll

take it from here." He reaches for the doll, and I hand it over,

because, of course, I would.

"Why? Why are you …?"

"The library moved the class to tomorrow, something

about plumbing repairs. I forgot to put it on my calendar, only

remembered after I left the store."

"Right, bummer." I nod again.

"Well, so, no intruders?" He gestures widely to the space.

"No intruders," I mumble.

"Good thing, that. Shall we go back downstairs?"

Another nod from me. I might as well write guilty on my

forehead with a permanent marker.

"Unless there is something you want to tell me?"

"No, no, I'm good, thanks. I'm sorry about …"

"It's okay. Don't worry about it." Mr. B smiles

reassuringly as he ushers me out. "Go ahead and re-open the

shop, I'll be right down."

There's a sound in my ears and it's growing in volume,

it sounds like the inside of a seashell, but I think it must be

my blood swooshing around louder and louder until it's all I

hear. My deafeningly loud guilty blood.

If I thought the week before was difficult, this one is downright unbearable. Outwardly, all things appear to be perfectly normal, all systems go, books are sold, quotidian pleasantries are exchanged. But just beneath the surface, there is a layer of tension thick enough to cut with a knife. And it's killing me. It's almost as if we are stuck acting out some play for the sake of some unseen audience. *I know he knows I know* loops infinitely through my mind. The impossible Möbius strip of logic and unimaginable consequences.

Those are my days. At night, there's a Greek chorus of angels pointing their accusing fingers and scream-whispering their threats. I'm lost and frightened and I have no one to talk to about it. I only ever had one person to talk to and now, how can I?

It's Mr. B that ends our standstill. He just looks at me one day and says, "We need to talk, Jared, don't we?"

I nod, gratefully. At long last, we'll shine the light on this toxic miasma lingering between us. See what we see.

"Come up to my place after we close. Just give me half an hour or so to settle in," he told me earlier today, and now I'm here, raising a timid hand to knock on his door. For the first time in my life, I'm afraid to talk to Mr. B, but talk we must.

He ushers me in with customary warmth, serves me tea and some of his endless supply of Girl Scout cookies. His kitchen is too small, and so his dining set takes up a corner in his living room. We sit down. The table is oak, solid, so are the chairs. Everything here is solid but my trembling, jelly-like insides.

"Jared, the other week. My class hadn't been moved, and

there were no plumbing repairs."

I let this sink in, the terrible weight of it.

"I know something's been going on with you," Mr. B starts after taking a slow sip of tea. As always, he is kind enough to take this off my shoulders by speaking first. "I notice things, you know. You haven't been sleeping well, you carry on about angels." *I thought I hadn't, not out loud.* "You read that terrible book —I saw it in your bag." *Thanks for that, angels.* "You snuck into my place under false pretenses. You tried stealing my property. And then you lied to me."

All true. I hang my head guiltily. What can I say? "I'm sorry," I offer, knowing it can't possibly be enough.

"Oh no." He waves it off. "I'm not looking for an apology. I care about you, kiddo. I want to know what's going through your mind. I want to help."

No, you don't, you really don't. If you did, you'd at best have me committed and at worst – what? – kill me? What am

I thinking here?

"I am sorry," I say in a stronger voice. "I had—" *Tell the truth and shame the devil, Jared.* "I had this lunch with Larry. I didn't plan it, he saw me outside and invited me, and he got in my head about this old Angelmaker case, and I've been having these, I don't know, visitations or nightmares, they call themselves angels, and they tell me terrible things. And I feel like I've been going crazy. Or I was afraid I was going crazy and didn't know what to do. And I just …"

I'm out of steam. So is my tea, and I sip it, putting effort into holding the cup in my shaking hands steady.

"What do they tell you, these angels?"

"They … they tell me that you are The Angelmaker. That you killed them all."

He nods, thoughtfully, like this is an ordinary tea and cookies conversation. "And what do they want from you?"

"They say they want justice."

"And what would that be to them?"

"I guess they want it to be out in the open, the truth. They say they can't rest until then."

"Ah." Mr. B eats one of the Lemon-Ups. Or maybe it's Lemonades. I never understood why Girl Scout brand would feature two such similar cookies.

"And what do you think?" he asks me after he washed down the cookies, never the one to talk with his mouth full.

"I don't know what to think anymore." It's the truth, I don't. Sitting here, over tea and cookies, talking it over, saying things out loud … well, it all seems insane, doesn't it? There is no possible way this wonderful, decent, generous man is a serial killer, was a serial killer. There are many possible ways that me, his accuser, a former addict with a history of mental issues and time on the streets served, has finally lost what was left of his sanity.

"What can I do to help?" he asks so kindly that I start crying. I don't want to. I can't remember the last time I cried. Maybe when Cherry died. I didn't even think I had this in my emotional repertoire anymore, and yet here I am, blubbering into my tea dregs.

"Oh, kiddo." Mr. B reaches across the table and puts his hand on mine. "It's okay, you're okay. You're just going through a rough patch."

These stupid tears, they just won't stop.

"Look, what if I were to tell you that the man known as The Angelmaker is dead and gone?"

I look up, he is blurry through my tears. "He is?"

"Yes."

I wipe my eyes as Mr. B says, "Let me tell you a story."

Right now, there's nothing I'd like more.

"Once upon a time, there was a man, an ordinary man who led an ordinary life. But secretly he dreamt terrible things, and he didn't know why. He had a nice upbringing, loving parents, a comfortable life—nothing about any of it could explain the nightmares he had, the frightening urges they breathed into him.

And so, one day he gave into them. He did what the nightmares had asked of him, and they abated. Then returned with their terrible demands and force him to act again. For a while, it went on that way, a vicious cycle, of sorts. And then one day it all just stopped. He didn't know why. He didn't dare question it, but one day, the dark dreams disappeared, and the urges went away. It was like waking up from a nightmare, one that seemed so real, he didn't even realize he was asleep. And just like that, it was over. He looked back at what he had done in horror, but he was no longer the same man who did all those things. He didn't even recognize that other man. And so, he did the only thing he could do, he confessed his crimes and did his best to move on, to put it all behind him, and be a good man.

"He knew there was nothing that could undo the terrible things he'd done, but he thought that if he led a good life, every day for all his days, if he did the right things, then maybe, just maybe, somehow, he would balance out the scales of justice in his own way. And so, he tried, every day, to be good, to be kind, to take care of others, to be a productive member of his community, to give back. All along hoping that it would be enough."

I wait, but he doesn't go on. I guess that's the end.

"And he lived happily ever after?" I ask.

"Not quite." Mr. B smiles sadly. "But close enough."

I'm confused. I don't know what to think, I don't know what to say. I feel ready to be taken away and sedated, whatever it takes to no longer be in this tumbling cycle of a headspace.

But I just have to ask, "Do you know that man, Mr. B?"

"No, Jared." He shakes his head ruefully. "I don't know that man at all. It was just a story."

We sit for a beat in uncomfortable silence.

"Are you going to be okay, kiddo?"

"No," I answer honestly, "I don't think so."

"Do you want some time off?"

I shake my head no.

"Do you, maybe, want to see someone?"

I was wondering how long that was going to take. Still, not an unreasonable question.

"I don't know," I say. I don't know anything anymore. I don't know what's real, I don't know what's true. I suppose that might be some definition of insanity. But wait …

"Why do you have that doll?"

"It's a memento."

"A memento?"

"Memento mori, have you heard of that? A reminder of the inevitability of death."

"It looks just like …" I can't say it, and so I angle my head vaguely in what I hope is an allusive manner.

"It looks like a great many things, from Native American totem art to a failed craft project."

He's right, of course. Or I think he's right. Or I would be thinking it if I was thinking clearly at the moment. All I can do is nod. All I do is nod.

"I should go," I say and make a move to get up. "You know, on second thought maybe a couple of days off would do me good."

"Of course. Take all the time you need. Do you want some cash?"

"No, no, I have the … I'm fine. I just need to rest and get my head on straight."

"Well, you know where I'll be. Whatever you need, just ask. Don't make me worry about you, kid. I'm too old to worry."

He smiles, there's some sadness there. I'm sad too. I finally have someone to worry about me, and *this* is what I do.

I depart, my shoulders bowed, my head low. Whatever weight Mr. B tried to lift off me has been replaced by guilt.

And something more, something like a profound fear of losing my mind. Like I'm in it, and I can't stop it, and no one can help me. Like being on a rollercoaster that's gone off the rails and is plummeting, plummeting …

I only go out once. To a corner I swore I'd never visit again, to see a person I swore I was done with. I come back with a full supply of chemical party supplies. Enough to turn off any brain, in overdrive mode or otherwise, enough to just shut down and be. It's all I want. A moment of peace, a moment of certainty, a respite from fear.

I'll be careful, I tell myself. I'll do it just this once. Use it as a reset and come back rebooted, a Jared 2.0 version. It's a stupid plan, maybe even a dangerous one, but it's all I got.

I'd lock myself in but there's no lock. Instead, I secure the door with a chair to the best of my ability.

And then I begin.

The angels come to me; I think. I can't be sure. They are angry, they say I failed them, they threaten to take matters into their own hands. I toast their intentions with cocktails of my own creation. And soon enough they fade away to whatever oblivion they had sprung from. And I drift toward the personal oblivion I so crave. No worries, no fears, I'm floating. It's pure magic. Why had I ever left this place? What made me think I could do better? This is so pure.

I don't know how much time I spend like this. The next thing I know for sure is a rude awakening—Mr. B hits my door, once, twice, until the chair I had edged there tumbles away, and then he rushes in. With him, a cloud of smoke.

He's screaming my name, I think. There's a wet towel wrapped around his face, muffling his voice. He drags me upwards, and my boneless body reluctantly follows. He continues dragging me as I try to regain feeling in my legs. Why am I not floating? Wasn't I just floating? What is this?

The bookstore is on fire. It's everywhere, hungrily licking the weathered spines, whispering promises of beautiful obliteration. Ashes to ashes.

I think I can hear the angels screaming. I try to turn around, to see them, but Mr. B is stronger than he looks, and I am so much weaker. I wish I could hear what they're saying. I don't know why—all I ever wanted was to silence them— but now I think it's important somehow. But I can't make out a single word.

We make it to the front door just as the fire trucks arrive. The sirens are ripping the night apart, the neighbors are pouring out onto the streets, clutching their robes, their faces glisten with fear or schadenfreude—there's no way to know. For that moment they are, all of them, gloriously alive.

A firefighter in full suit and helmet reaches for me, relieves Mr. B of me. I'm choking on the smoke, and I still can't walk on my own accord. I look back and see Mr. B watching the store. My eyes catch a movement in the front, it's the angels—ghost-like, translucent girls, not demons at all, I don't know what I was thinking. They look happy, they look free. They look … vindicated.

Where were they this entire time? In the building's foundation? In its walls? Or just— *always*—in my unsteady addled mind? Will I ever know?

I watch Mr. B start back toward the store. That can't be right. I want to scream in protest but can't get enough air. Why isn't anyone helping him? Why isn't anyone noticing? It's bedlam all around, the greatest burning of the books since the Third Reich, surely. The firefighters are doing their best to prevent the flames from leaping over to the neighboring houses. I try to go after him, but I succeed only as far as breaking free of the first response person trying to check my vitals, before falling to the ground immediately. On my knees, a penitent, I watch Mr. B collapse at the store's entrance, half in half out. Of both worlds to the end.

I think I see the ghostly hands reaching for him then, but I can't say for sure, because at last, my broken mind mercifully draws the curtain.

It was only smoke inhalation, they told me. I was okay to go. They must have noted the amount of junk in my system but said nothing about it. Uncaring or dismissive or simply inured to it all.

Mr. B died of a massive heart attack. They said it was instant as if I'm meant to find some comfort there. I try, but in the end, my guilt outweighs it all.

They told me it was some faulty electric wiring that started a fire, just one of those things, they said. I don't believe them. But then again, they wouldn't believe me if I told them my version of the events either.

I go back to the store. There is almost nothing left—books make for good fuel. Scorched ruins; somewhere among them, my meager possessions, my small savings fund, my favorite books. My clothes. I don't even have a suit to wear to the funeral. I'll go as I am; I know he wouldn't care. I'll say "I'm sorry" a thousand times. I'll ask for forgiveness I don't deserve. I'll thank him for saving my life, twice. I'll tell him I understand, I understand now, even though it's too late.

My third act will be distinctly less impressive than my second. I have nothing; I have nowhere to go. I'm right back to where I was when I met Mr. B. There was a person I was in-between, I know, but it's already beginning to seem like a dream. Because we change, don't we? With every act, we change. We are not the people stepping into the river hoping to find it unchanged, we are the river. I am forever changed now.

I'll find a street corner. I'll sit and wait. Someday, maybe, I'll have someone in my life again. I won't have much to offer them, but I can always tell them a story.

Mia Dalia is an internationally published author, a lifelong reader, and a longtime reviewer of all things fantastic, thrilling, scary, and strange.

Her short fiction has been published by online by Night Terror Novels, 50-word stories, Flash Fiction Magazine, Pyre Magazine, Tales from the Moonlit Path and in print anthologies by Sunbury Press, HellBound Press, Black Ink Fiction, Dragon Roost Press, Unsettling Reads, Moon, Anthology of Lunar Horror, Phobica Books, Psycho Toxin Press, Wandering Wave Press, Bullet Points vol. 3, Critical Blast,Sinister Smile Press, , Exploding Head Press ,and DraculaBeyondStoker Magazine.

Her fiction will be featured in the upcoming anthologies by Nightshade Press, Book Slayer Press, RebellionLIT, Grendel Press, Phobica Books, CelticFrog Press, and Crystal

Lake Publishing.

Mia's Noir tales have been published by Mystery Magazine and Bang! Noir Anthology from Headshot Press.

Her short fiction has been featured by narrative podcasts such as Zoetic Press' Alphanumeric and Tales to Terrify.

She has released two novellas with PsychoToxin Press: *Tell Me a Story* and *Discordant*.

Her debut novel, *Estate Sale*, was published in April of 2023 to rave reviews.

Mia's first collection of horror and thrillers, *Smile So Red and Other Tales of Madness*, was released in January 2024 by Anuci Press.

She makes her science fiction debut with *Arrakoth*, due out from Spaceboy Books in the summer of 2024.

Her second novel, *Haven*, will be released by CamCat Books in the fall of 2024.

Find her at

Official website: https://daliaverse.wixsite.com/author

Twitter: @ Dalia_Verse

FB: DaliaVerse

Instagram: daliaverse

https://linktr.ee/daliaverse

Acknowledgments

Dear reader. This is for you, if you're the sort that sticks around for the credits. First off, thank you. Thank you so much! There are plenty other things you could be doing with your time and/or plenty other books you could be reading, but you chose mine, and I am grateful. I hope you were entertained, disturbed, delighted. All that.

I'm always curious to know what inspires the stories I read. So I figured it's only fair to return the favor now that I'm a writer.
Tell Me a Story was inspired by my love of books and bookstores. But, because my mind tends to veer toward the dark side, the story ended up having ghosts and a serial killer. What I really wanted was to explore the true meaning of second chances. It's a subject I'm always coming back to and will feature again in an upcoming work.
I'd like to view people's personalities as multifaceted and believe we are more than the things we've done. What my characters believe is another story altogether.

I'd like to thank the following:

Arthur Shattuck O'Keefe for his amazing advice, edits, and all-around awesomeness. Do yourself a favor and read his book, *The Spirit Phone*.

Tony Anuci of Anuci Press for giving this story about second chances a second chance to shine and for being a bright star among small presses.

Gary Goodman's memoir, *The Last Bookseller, A Life in the Rare Book Trade*, for inspiration and information.

My superfan, Atticus Morton, for always believing.

BETA readers who helped me finetune the story.

Davida De La Harpe Golden, the speedreading demon.
Go raibh maith agat as gach rud.

All the wonderful authors who have taken the time to read and blurb my book.

And most importantly, my beautiful wife, Chelsea, who has always made me feel like a storyteller.

If you enjoyed this book, kindly take a moment to leave a review on Amazon and/or Goodreads.

Tell your friends.

Shout it from the rooftops.

It'll make the author very happy and will do wonders for your karma.

Until next time …